Jasi

He imagined seeing Mattie around town, pregnant and glowing.

With some other man's baby. And Orren's gut twisted cold. He felt as if a weight had dropped onto his chest. He couldn't quite breathe, and he couldn't seem to feel his own heartbeat. Mattie and some other man. No way. No way could he stand that.

He couldn't even picture Mattie with someone else. She'd never been with anyone else. He knew that as surely as he knew his own name. And he knew, too, that when Mattie went to a man, he would be her one and her only. He knew he couldn't let that man be anyone but him.

Damn if he wasn't going to have to marry that girl.

THIS SIDE OF HEAVEN:
Beloved author Arlene James weaves another heartwarming tale of the residents of Duncan, Oklahoma.

Dear Reader,

Unforgettable Bride, by bestselling author Annette Broadrick, is May's VIRGIN BRIDES selection, *and* the much-requested spin-off to her DAUGHTERS OF TEXAS series. Rough, gruff rodeo star Bobby Metcalf agreed to a quickie marriage—sans honeymoon!—with virginal Casey Carmichael. But four years later, he's still a married man—one intent on being a husband to Casey in every sense....

Fabulous author Arlene James offers the month's FABULOUS FATHERS title, *Falling for a Father of Four.* Orren Ellis was a single dad to a brood of four, so hiring sweet Mattie Kincaid seemed the perfect solution. Until he found himself falling for this woman he could never have.... Stella Bagwell introduces the next generation of her bestselling TWINS ON THE DOORSTEP series. In *The Rancher's Blessed Event,* an ornery bronc rider must open his heart both to the woman who'd betrayed him...and her child yet to be born.

Who can resist a sexy, stubborn cowboy—particularly when he's your husband? Well, Taylor Cassidy tries in Anne Ha's *Long, Tall Temporary Husband.* But will she succeed? And Sharon De Vita's irresistible trio, LULLABIES AND LOVE, continues with *Baby with a Badge,* where a bachelor cop finds a baby in his patrol car...and himself in desperate need of a woman's touch! Finally, new author C.J. Hill makes her commanding debut with a title that sums it up best: *Baby Dreams and Wedding Schemes.*

Romance has everything you need from new beginnings to tried-and-true favorites. Enjoy each and every novel this month, and every month!

Warm Regards!

Joan Marlow Golan

Joan Marlow Golan
Senior Editor, Silhouette Romance

Please address questions and book requests to:
Silhouette Reader Service
U.S.: 3010 Walden Ave., P.O. Box 1325, Buffalo, NY 14269
Canadian: P.O. Box 609, Fort Erie, Ont. L2A 5X3

Arlene James

FALLING FOR A FATHER OF FOUR

Silhouette
ROMANCE™
Published by Silhouette Books
America's Publisher of Contemporary Romance

SILHOUETTE BOOKS

ISBN 0-373-19295-9

FALLING FOR A FATHER OF FOUR

This edition published by arrangement with Harlequin Books S.A.

Printed in U.S.A.

Books by Arlene James

Silhouette Romance

City Girl #141
No Easy Conquest #235
Two of a Kind #253
A Meeting of Hearts #327
An Obvious Virtue #384
Now or Never #404
Reason Enough #421
The Right Moves #446
Strange Bedfellows #471
The Private Garden #495
The Boy Next Door #518
Under a Desert Sky #559
A Delicate Balance #578
The Discerning Heart #614
Dream of a Lifetime #661
Finally Home #687
A Perfect Gentleman #705
Family Man #728
A Man of His Word #770
Tough Guy #806
Gold Digger #830
Palace City Prince #866
**The Perfect Wedding* #962
**An Old-Fashioned Love* #986
**A Wife Worth Waiting For* #974
Mail-Order Brood #1024
**The Rogue Who Came To Stay* #1061
**Most Wanted Dad* #1144
Desperately Seeking Daddy #1186
**Falling for a Father of Four* #1295

Silhouette Special Edition

A Rumor of Love #664
Husband in the Making #776
With Baby in Mind #869
Child of Her Heart #964
The Knight, the Waitress and the Toddler #1131

*This Side of Heaven

ARLENE JAMES

grew up in Oklahoma and has lived all over the South. In 1976 she married "the most romantic man in the world." The author enjoys traveling with her husband, but writing has always been her chief pastime.

Fabulous Fathers

THOUGHTS ON FATHERHOOD:

To my children,

I'm so proud of you four. Each of you in your own way has a deep, instinctive understanding of love. You, Chaz, eldest and only son, understand that love is responsibility, which you so willingly and ably accept. For bright Jean Marie, love is to be tightly grasped and defended. My Yancy doll has always known that love is for happily sharing. And my sweet baby Candy Sue carries love to us all in every smile and cuddle.

Because of you four, I've always had reason to count my blessings. You've gotten me through some tough times. You brought Mattie to us. (She says that we make her complete, but we know that she was the missing part of our family.) Never forget that it has always been and will always be you who make me what I am, a happy father of four. Maybe one day before long I'll even be a happy father of five…or six…or… Who knows? And who can blame me, when every one of you has brought me such joy, for wanting more?

I will always love you. Chaz. Jean Marie. Yancy. Candy Sue. Wherever you eventually go, whatever you may or may not do, whomever you will become, I will always love you. Always.

Daddy

Chapter One

"Get down, you big baby, and get outta my way!"

Jean Marie shoved at her younger sister, not hard enough to really send her over the edge of the counter and crashing to the floor, but hard enough to let her know that she meant business. Sitting at the kitchen table, Orren covered the mouthpiece of the telephone receiver and counted to ten, striving for patience as four-year-old Yancy Kay wailed and called for her "bubby," Chaz. All of eight, Chaz was the family hero, and Orren knew that he depended on his son too much, but wasn't he doing everything in his power to try to take some of the weight off of those slender shoulders? Not, however, at the moment. He nodded at Chaz, who disgustedly reached past Yancy's tormentor, their six-year-old sister Jean Marie, and heaved Yancy off the counter, against which Jean Marie had pushed a chair in order to prepare her specialty of buttered crackers for an afternoon snack.

"You don't have to be such a meanie," Chaz scolded in a low mutter.

Deeply offended, Jean Marie threw the knife with which

she was working into the sink, where it clattered noisily among the other dishes. Yancy yowled, and Orren's caller hung up. He couldn't blame her. No woman in her right mind would willingly walk into this lion's den. Orren put his head in his hands and sighed. "Well, that's another one we can forget about."

Repentant, Yancy stuck her thumb in her mouth and laid her tousled golden-blond head on Chaz's shoulder. "I'm sorry, Dad," the boy said. Then he turned his attention to the four-year-old wrapped around him. "You shouldn't have climbed up on the counter, Yancy. The apples are all gone, anyway."

"I'll get some more when I go to the store," Orren promised tiredly, getting up to hang up the phone. Trying to sound reasonable, he turned a look at redheaded Jean Marie. "You shouldn't talk so ugly to your baby sister, Red."

"She ain't the baby," Jean Marie retorted unconcernedly, taking another clean knife from the drawer. "She just acts like it."

She was right. Three-year-old Sweetums, otherwise known as Candy Sue, was still enjoying her afternoon nap, her curly, pale blond head lying on his pillow even as they spoke, but that wasn't the point. "You still shouldn't be so cross with her. She just wanted an apple."

"We ain't got any apples," Jean Marie said, "and she was gonna fall on her durned fool head."

"Watch your mouth!" Orren snapped, despair sitting on him like a big mother hen brooding a chick. He'd had two calls on the ad, and both had hung up after hearing how many kids they'd be expected to sit and the unmistakable sounds of the chaos that reigned over his household. Fourteen bucks wasted and a day of work lost for nothing. What was he going to do tomorrow when he had to show up for work? He was scared to death to leave them alone, but how could he work and care for them, too?

He looked at Chaz, sighing. "You may have to go back

to the day care," he said, and winced as both Jean Marie and Yancy screamed protests, Jean Marie with several words she shouldn't even have known, Yancy with her usual howl. He pointed a stern finger at Jean Marie. "Go to your room, young lady. I won't have you talking like that."

"I hate that old day care!" she yelled. "That Porter woman'll call welfare on us!"

"No, she won't," Chaz said resignedly. "She's onto your tricks and lies now."

Orren shook his head, recalling all the ways Jean Marie had sought to get herself and her siblings barred from the day care center: the strawberry jelly rashes, the hole-riddled underwear and socks, the tall tales about deadly diseases and strange curses. He wasn't at all certain Mrs. Porter would take them full time. After-school care had been difficult enough. But what other choice did he have now that school was out? He started planning his plea and tried not to think about what it was going to cost, especially since the hours would mean cutting back on the side jobs he took to make a little extra.

"Get on to your room," he said to Jean Marie as the phone rang again. She threw herself off the chair and pounded away, slamming doors in her wake. Orren sent a look to Chaz as he reached for the receiver of the wall-mounted phone near the door. "Check on the baby. If the phone doesn't wake her, Jean Marie will." He snatched up the receiver in the middle of a second ring. "Hello."

A bright voice at the other end of the line said, "Hi, my name is Matilda Kincaid."

Mattie hung up the phone and smiled in satisfaction. Mr. Orren Ellis sounded frankly desperate. She was welcome to come out and interview even if she wasn't the grandmotherly type specified in his ad, and the sooner the better. Right away, in fact. They could talk about the kids and the other duties once she got there. All she had to do was hit

Bois d'arc off the 81 Bypass and follow it past the old cemetery. It was the beige and white house on the right, with the For Sale sign standing up close to the road. Come to the carport door. The For Sale sign was for the acreage and not the house.

Mattie rolled off her bed onto the floor, stabbed her feet into sandals and snatched up the hairbrush on the dressing table beneath the window. Yanking several strokes through her long dark hair, she dropped the brush into the small denim backpack that had replaced her purse during her first year of college at Oklahoma State in Stillwater. Free for the summer, she was ready for a job and the slow pace of the hot summertime in Duncan. She'd be happier still if she never had to set eyes again on the hallowed old halls of higher education, but after only two years at the university, it was doubtful her father would hear of her leaving college.

As if conjured by her thoughts, she jerked open her bedroom door to find Evans Kincaid standing with fist raised to knock, his tan uniform as crisp as his badge was shiny, despite a full day put in as one of Duncan's finest. Tall and fit in his mid-forties, his inky hair trimmed close to his head, he was the quintessential police officer.

"Hello, sweetheart! How was your day?" He bent and kissed her on the cheek.

"Oh, fine. Amy's out back lighting the grill."

"Ah. Well, I'll run out and tell her I'm home. You, however, have company."

He grinned, his leaf green eyes twinkling with delight. Mattie almost groaned aloud. That look could mean anything from a new puppy to a "playmate," all designed to delight the little girl she no longer was. Poor Dad! He just couldn't accept that she was no longer a child. At nineteen-going-on-twenty, Mattie was far more mature than most of her contemporaries. Truth be told, she felt decades older than the young people with whom she shared classes at OSU. She supposed it had something to do with losing her mother at so young an age and stepping into the role of housekeeper during the years before her father found Amy, his sweet second wife, who used to be their next-door neighbor. She counted Amy more good friend than stepmother and loved her—if for no other reason—for making her father happy and for occasionally running interference when Evans Kincaid became too obsessively "parental."

Evans pointed her in the direction of the living room and went on out through the kitchen to kiss his wife. Mattie sighed and took herself off to greet her unknown guest. She stifled a second groan and rolled her eyes upon discovering Brick Carter studying the display of her father's medals and awards won in the line of duty. Brick swung around, freckled face splitting in a wide grin.

"Hey, Mat!" Brick had an annoying habit of shortening everyone's name to a single syllable like his own. His carrot red hair had been shorn so close that the pink of his scalp shone through, and the prominence of his front teeth gave him a rabbity look. "How long you been home?"

"Just since Wednesday," Mattie answered, as if that explained why she hadn't seen him, when in truth she'd avoided him like the plague, even sneaking out of church early to avoid an accidental meeting. "Congratulations on your graduation."

Brick stuck out his thin chest, his hands jingling the change in his chino pockets. "Thanks. It sure feels good to have that sheepskin!"

"What are you going to do now that you've finished university?"

He shrugged. "I don't know. Take some time off, I guess. I'm kind of young to get tied down to a job already, and Mom wants me to think about grad school. I'll probably do that. Right now, though, I just want to have some fun! Hey, how about taking in an early movie and—"

"Sorry," Mattie interrupted. "I was just on my way out. I have a job interview."

"A job interview?" This came from behind her, her father's voice.

She turned, masking her irritation with a smile. "That's right, and I really have to go. Mr. Ellis is expecting me."

"Ellis?" Evans turned the name over in his mind. "Can't say I know any Ellis."

Mattie shot a pleading look over his shoulder at her stepmother. "Must be law-abiding," Amy quipped with a wink at Mattie.

"What kind of job is it?" Evans wanted to know.

"Baby-sitting," Mattie said easily, not yet ready to reveal that it was full time.

"Oh, well, then, that's all right. But, honey, you really don't have to work. You have your allowance and—"

"Dad!" Mattie closed her eyes in humiliation. "I'm not a child. I don't need or want an allowance. I'm perfectly capable of earning my own way. If you hadn't insisted I come home, I could have moved into a secretarial job in Stillwater."

Evans waved that away with a deprecating chuckle. "You don't want to be a secretary."

Mattie had to bite her tongue to keep from asking how he knew what she wanted to be when she didn't know herself—except that the idea of working with children did hold a good deal more appeal than remaining with the real estate firm for which she'd worked part time last semester. In fact, she hoped the Ellis household contained a number of children, two or three, at least. With another pleading look at Amy, she said, "I really have to go now," and whirled away, flipping a wave in farewell. "So long, Brick. Say hello to your sister for me. Bye, Dad."

"Hey, what about dinner?" Evans called after her, moving into the doorway.

"Oh, don't worry about me!" she called back, hurrying down the walk toward her car. "I'll get something later. Maybe Brick will want to stay."

Evans frowned as she all but skipped down the walkway.

He almost called her back, but his wife's hand on his forearm stayed him. A glance in her direction told him that he was in danger of becoming the heavy-handed father again. With a sigh, he closed the door and turned back into the living room. "Well, Brick, how about it? Want to stay for dinner?"

Brick shrugged. "Sure!" Brick's personal theory, well known to all acquainted with him, was that he ought never to turn down a free meal. Evans smiled lamely and went to change his clothes.

"She's here!" Chaz announced, moving away from the kitchen sink where he'd kept watch through the window. Orren glanced up in time to see the late-model red two-door turn into the drive. It was a make with a good reputation for safety and dependability, yet had a racy look about it. A good choice for a second car, a single person more intent on value than prestige, or a teenager with particularly careful parents. He prayed it wasn't a teenager—these kids of his would eat the average teenager alive—but he didn't have time to watch from a distance as she got out of the car and moved toward the door. Instead, he ran across the hallway into his bedroom, where he dumped another armload of junk, kicking it out of the way as he wrestled the door closed and ran back to the living area. She knocked just as he moved on into the kitchen.

Motioning for Chaz to get out of the way, Orren crossed to the door, where he paused and pulled a deep, calming breath, drying his sweating palms on his jeaned thighs. He opened the door to a petite cutie with enormous green eyes and dark hair falling down her back in a sleek sheet. She wore a gauzy yellow blouse over a white tank top and a faded denim miniskirt, yellow sandals on her small, bare feet. She had that firm, fit look of the well-endowed teenager, but something about her face hinted that she might be older. Perhaps it was the carefully applied lipstick in a sensible shade of peach or the hint of blush across her high cheekbones. Whatever it was, it gave him a glimmer of hope.

"Mr. Ellis?" she asked. "I'm Matilda Kincaid."

Nodding, he backed out of the doorway. "Miss Kincaid. Won't you come in?"

She stepped up into the house and shrugged off the backpack she carried slung over one shoulder. Looking around in blatant curiosity, she spied Chaz and moved in his direction, hand extended. "Hello. I'm Mattie."

"This is my son, Chaz," Orren said, proudly dropping his hands onto Chaz's stout shoulders as Chaz stiffly placed his hand in Mattie's.

"Pleased to meet you, Chaz." She smiled and lifted her gaze to Orren's, the shock of those emerald eyes rocking him back a little. "Are there others? Children, I mean."

She sounded almost eager, but Orren wasn't taking any chances. She was young, but she handled herself with a certain maturity. He wouldn't count her out until they'd talked—and he wasn't about to scare her off, either. He nodded smoothly and smiled down at Chaz. "Son, why don't you go and get Sweetums?"

Chaz's pale blue eyes signaled his approval of this particular maneuver. Few females could resist the curly-headed little moppet with eyes the color of a summer sky. They'd spring Yancy and Jean Marie on her later, if things got that far. As Chaz went off to fetch his baby sister, Orren pulled out a chair from the kitchen table.

"Won't you sit down, Miss Kincaid?"

"Yes, thank you."

She hung her backpack on the back of the chair and gracefully lowered herself onto the seat, tucking her little skirt around her legs. Nice legs, Orren noticed, for a girl her age, that was. And perhaps finding out her exact age ought to be the first order of business. Counselling himself to patience, Orren doggedly observed the niceties.

"Can I get you anything? A cup of tea, maybe?"

"Oh, no, thank you. And please call me Mattie." Her

smile was slightly mocking as she added, "Miss Kincaid is my father's maiden aunt."

He felt himself smiling in response. "Well, you're obviously no old maid, so Mattie it is. My name's Orren, by the way. We can save Mr. Ellis for the fellows down at the shop. The mister is a way of reminding them who's boss."

"You're young to be anyone's boss, aren't you?" she said smoothly.

He was shocked, and not just because he felt a hundred most days, but because she had so neatly turned the tables on him. He knew what it was like to be young and struggling. The world was full of folks who thought you had to be skimming forty to do anything worthwhile, and woe to the man who set out to prove himself capable before then. He just hadn't expected the question from this little slip of a female. He pulled out a chair and dropped into it, saying defensively, "I'm twenty-eight."

Her dark, slender brows rose in tandem. "My goodness, you were awful young when Chaz was born, then, weren't you? What is he, nine or ten?"

"Eight." Orren retorted. "Chaz is eight. He won't be nine until November."

"Ah. Then you were an expectant father at my age," she announced, beaming at him.

Orren blinked, wondering how he'd lost control of this interview. The same way he'd lost control of his life, apparently—without even realizing it. A hushed squabble in the hallway alerted him to more trouble in the making. "Excuse me," he said, rising and edging that way. Before he could get there, though, Jean Marie slithered through the open doorway, evading Chaz's grasp. She glared at him mulishly, pushing her blazing red hair out of her face. He'd told her pointedly to brush it, but she seemed to think that taming her hair was the height of indignity. She targeted Mattie Kincaid with a frown that abruptly upended itself. This was no old meanie. This was a pliable, hoodwinkable youngster! Jean Marie beamed and headed for her. Orren caught her about the shoulders and redirected her toward the tattered brown tweed couch, saying, "This is Jean Marie. We call her Red, for obvious reasons."

Mattie smiled at the girl. "Hello, Jean Marie. What beautiful hair you have."

Jean Marie gaped and shoved at the unruly mess. "I don't, neither."

"Yes, you do. I think it's very pretty."

Jean Marie pulled a face at her father, all but sticking out her tongue, as if to say, "So there!"

Chaz edged into the room with the baby on his hip, an apologetic look on his face. Candy Sue rubbed her eyes sleepily, and Orren hurried to introduce her. "This here is Sweetums, uh, Candy Sue. She's three, and Jean Marie here is six."

"What a doll!" Mattie exclaimed, holding out her arms. Chaz gratefully delivered Candy Sue, who went to Mattie without the slightest hesitation. Why should she balk when she'd been passed from stranger to stranger her whole little life, Orren mused, fighting back the anger such thoughts always brought with them. Just then Yancy bolted into the room, bounced off the edge of the armchair and threw her arms around Chaz's hips to stop and steady herself. Her thumb went immediately into her mouth. Her golden-blond hair had been pulled ruthlessly back from her face with a green plastic barrette, Jean Marie's handiwork, no doubt. Chaz scolded her softly.

"You were s'posed to wait!"

"Ah wai'ed," she said around her thumb.

"You were s'posed to wait till I come and got you!" he hissed desperately.

Orren cast an anxious glance at the prospective babysitter. Mattie, however, laughed and rocked forward onto the edge of her chair, Candy Sue cuddled in her lap. "And what's your name, sweetheart?"

Yancy pulled her thumb from her mouth and answered importantly, "I's Yancy Kay."

"And how old are you, Yancy Kay?"

Yancy held up four fingers, carefully folding back her wet thumb.

Mattie spread a smile over them, saying, "Is this everyone?"

Orren nodded morosely. "This is the lot."

Mattie squirmed in her chair as if just barely able to contain her glee. "Let me see if I've got everyone down." Her gaze lit on Chaz. "Chaz is the oldest at eight, and a very good big brother, too, I'm guessing."

Yancy threw both arms around him again, exclaiming worshipfully, "Bubby!"

Mattie laughed. Orren joined her belatedly, wondering what she found so delightful. Chaz just looked confused. Mattie turned her smile on the sulky one.

"Jean Marie of the beautiful hair is six," she recited, "and I'm guessing she has a temper to go along with that blaze of red."

Jean Marie stuck out her bottom lip and folded her arms emphatically, proclaiming Mattie correct, but her vivid blue eyes gleamed with secret delight. Orren shook his head. Mattie went on to the thumb sucker.

"Miss Yancy Kay is four and loves being babied by her big brother."

Yancy responded by trying to squeeze Chaz in two.

Mattie wrapped her arms around placid Candy Sue and tickled her lightly, saying, "And Candy Sue is everybody's three-year-old Sweetums." Candy Sue giggled that delightful baby laugh that could still lift Orren's beleaguered spirits. Mattie laughed with her, then hugged her hard.

Jean Marie got up and walked over to Mattie's chair, leaning against it in disarming familiarity. "If you come work for us, will you try to make me brush my hair?" she asked challengingly.

Mattie smiled. "Nope." Jean Marie gaped for a second time. Mattie added, "But you won't get my special snacks if you don't."

Jean Marie clamped her mouth shut in a frown. "What special snacks?"

Mattie shrugged. "Brush your hair, and you'll see."

Jean Marie scowled. Maybe this one wasn't quite so easily managed, after all.

Orren had to hide a smile. He waded through the children toward the table, saying to Chaz, "Son, take the girls out back to play while I talk to Miss, um, Mattie."

"Is that your name?" Jean Marie demanded, eyes narrowed. "Mattie?"

"Yes, it is," came the smooth answer. "*Miss* Mattie to you. It's short for Matilda."

Put firmly in her place, Jean Marie brought her hands to her hips and announced baldly, "I don't like her."

Orren glared and opened his mouth to lay down a scathing scold, but Mattie Kincaid, in her cool, unflappable style, beat him to it. "Now, Jean Marie," she said calmly, "you might as well know right now that those bullying tactics won't work with me. My father's a policeman, you see, and he taught me that bullies are usually more scared than anyone else and they act all tough to hide it. So what are you scared of, Jean Marie, a little old hairbrush? Or maybe you'd rather have some warty old witch who'd spank you and put you to bed without your dinner instead of making you delicious snacks and keeping things neat around here, hmm?"

Jean Marie's mouth was hanging open again. Clearly at a loss, she spun and ran out of the room. Chaz's eyes were big as saucers, but no bigger than his father's. Orren had seldom seen his prickly daughter routed so easily, and he frankly didn't know whether to be optimistic or worried about it! He turned away, trying to make up his mind about the confounding Matilda Kincaid, his hand lighting on the back of his neck.

Mattie, meanwhile, smoothly took control. Calling Chaz forward with a crooking finger, she put Candy Sue on her feet and motioned for him to take the two younger girls out as his father had instructed. Casting curious glances in his father's direction, Chaz silently complied, herding the girls ahead of him. When Orren turned back around, Mattie was sitting alone at the table, her hands folded in her lap. He shot a surprised look around the room, frowned, and leaned forward to place both hands flat on the table.

"How old are you?" he asked bluntly, determined to maintain control this time.

Mattie smiled serenely. "Nineteen, the same age you were when you made Chaz."

Orren's frown deepened. "Nineteen's young to watch over four kids—and to be so damned direct!"

Her smile never faltered. "I'll be twenty soon, if it really makes any difference. And it's true, isn't it? You were just nineteen when Chaz's mother was expecting him."

He couldn't deny it, so instead he got defensive about it. "Girl, you've got some brass!" She ignored him, craning her neck to get a good look around, though what there was to look at, he couldn't guess.

"Where is she?"

"Who?"

Her gaze was completely undisturbed. "Your wife."

He felt like he'd been coldcocked. "I don't have one!"

She looked askance at that. "Those children didn't spring out of the ground."

Orren threw up his arms. "She ran away with a rodeo bum! Anything else you want to know?"

She shook her head, but whether in answer to his sarcastic question or in response to his ill-natured revelation, he didn't know. She looked him squarely in the eye and said, "I can start right away."

Defeated, he plopped down in the chair he'd vacated earlier and sighed. "I bet you lead your daddy a merry chase."

Mattie nodded unrepentantly. "He thinks I'm still twelve, which is how old I was when my mother died."

Orren put his head in his hands. "I don't know whether

to slit my throat now or hold out a few years in hopes my own girls will run off with circus performers."

"You don't mean that," Mattie told him, as if he didn't already know it.

He dropped his hands and gave her a hard look. "Does your father know you're here?"

"Of course."

"How do you suppose he'll feel about you working for a single man my age?"

She shrugged. "Hard to tell. He might assume you're too old to be attractive to me."

He couldn't believe he'd heard that right. *"What?"*

She ignored him as if he hadn't spoken and went on. "Or he might assume you're too old to be *attracted* to me. Either way, I'll be too young in his mind. But, it's a baby-sitting job, and he'll think that's appropriate, so it shouldn't be any problem, really. If he hedges, I'll enlist my step-mother's aid. She's never had children so she doesn't have these parental hang-ups. And if he outright forbids it, we'll have a screaming fight. Then I'll take the job anyway, because it's what I want, and I am, after all, over eighteen. I have two years of college, by the way."

Orren just stared at her for a second. "I think I will cut my throat."

She got up from the table and said, "Can I look around?"

"No!"

She threw out a slender hip and propped her hand on it. Yes, indeed, she was over eighteen. But she was still a baby. Especially compared to Gracie. He frowned. Now why had he done that, compared her to Grace? She folded her arms and asked baldly, "So how long has she been gone?"

He nearly hit his chin on the table. Little shocker. Well, if she wanted the dirty details, he'd give them to her. He got up and put his hands flat on the table, drilling her with his baby blues. "Two years and seven months." He waited a beat and added, "A week and three days."

She batted her lashes at him. "Candy Sue was just a baby."

"An infant," he admitted. "I had to put her on a bottle." Let her digest that.

She was outraged. A nursing mother had abandoned her baby, not to mention three other children and a husband! Then she started looking for acceptable reasons. "She must've been young when you married."

"Older than me," he said flatly, "but that didn't keep me from getting her pregnant. Four times."

Miss Matilda Kincaid lifted her chin a notch. "You're trying to embarrass me."

"And succeeding," he admitted, looking at the splotches of color spreading across her cheeks. "Maybe that'll teach you not to go around asking nosy questions."

"Is there a better way to find out what I want to know?" she retorted saucily.

He grinned. Damned if she didn't have him there. "You ever hear that curiosity killed the cat?"

She rolled her eyes. "It's pretty obvious I'm not a cat, and it wouldn't be very responsible of me to walk into a situation blind, would it?"

He scratched his chin at that. "Guess not. You've just got an awful frank way about you."

"Yes, I do. Now, is the job mine or not?"

He shook his head, chuckling, and said the one thing guaranteed to get her dander up. "Well, I don't know. I'll have to talk to your dad first, clear it with him."

The color in her face blossomed to full red as she struggled to tamp down her temper. It took several seconds, actually, of breathing through her mouth and working her jaw, but she finally got it in hand. That hip flew out again, and she was clearly fuming, but she managed a nearly polite, "Fine."

He went to the phone, figuring it would be dangerous for him to laugh outright. "What's his name?"

"Evans Kincaid."

"I want you to know I'm doing this because you said earlier that he's a police officer, which seems a good recommendation. Are you really nineteen?"

"Yes!"

"What's the telephone number?"

She ground it out through bared teeth, and he punched it into the telephone. The conversation was fairly short. Kincaid was obviously pleased that he'd been consulted. It marked Orren, he said, as a conscientious father himself. Orren politely but honestly explained that he was divorced and fairly desperate as he hadn't generated much interest in the position, the hours being tricky and *some* housekeeping being required. Actually he was hoping for more than some housekeeping, but he wouldn't mention that. He couldn't exactly demand it, considering the wages he was able to pay, and he knew he had no right to expect it. Since his days off as manager of the car repair shop were Sunday and Monday, he pointed out that he would expect Mattie to work Saturday. He didn't say that he could easily keep her busy seven days a week by taking small jobs on the side, but he was hoping Mattie would welcome the extra money as much as he did. At any rate, Kincaid made it plain that he would not approve of Mattie working Sundays, and Orren made special note of it, figuring that Kincaid was a religious man who wouldn't take kindly to having his little girl's ears scorched more than they already had been.

Mattie, her father promised, was great with kids and a hard worker. She knew her way around a house, too, having pretty much taken over the domestic duties after her mother died. "She's a great little organizer," he said proudly, "and neat as a pin."

Orren looked around at his hastily cleared combination kitchen and living room and wondered if Mattie would last a week here in this madhouse with her penchant for order and neatness. He could only hope.

"Between you and me," Kincaid went on, "I think, she's felt a little displaced since I remarried. She and Amy are fast friends, but I've noticed that Mattie is a little restless and uncertain when she's home from school. This might be good for her."

"I hope so," Orren said warmly, but privately he had his doubts. He loved his kids, but sometimes he thought he'd go stark raving mad. It was always one crisis after another around this place, and there was never enough money, what with the cost of child care and all. Sometimes he wanted to just walk out, not forever, but maybe long enough to get blind drunk on occasion. Still, he couldn't afford that much beer, and he sure couldn't afford the hard liquor for it, not with someone constantly outgrowing shoes or coming up with ear infections and such. He hung up the phone and turned to take the new sitter's measure one more time.

"You heard?"

She nodded. "When do I start?"

He was surprised, really, that she still wanted to. Maybe she didn't understand everything involved. "I work ten to seven, five and sometimes six days a week. I'll try to get breakfast for the kids before I go, but lunch and dinner are part of your job."

"All right."

"I can fend for myself," he went on, "but the kids have got to eat regular meals."

"I understand. I don't see any reason for you to do without, though, considering I'm going to be cooking anyway."

That was good news. "Well, dinner, maybe," he conceded gratefully. "I usually skip lunch, though sometimes someone will take me out."

She shrugged. "What about the grocery shopping?"

He hedged that. "I try to do it on Mondays, but sometimes it's Tuesday evening before I can get to it.'' *Or Wednesday,* he thought. *Or Thursday. If at all.*

''I'd rather do it myself, if you'll give me a budget,'' she said. ''I prefer to make out weekly menus and shop with a list. It cuts down on impulse buying and makes use of things that might otherwise go to waste. I do the shopping on Mondays, floors on Tuesday, bathrooms on Wednesday, dusting on Thursday, and laundry on Friday, though I suppose my Monday will be Tuesday, so we can push everything back a day, if you want.''

He couldn't believe it, not coming from this small, delicate girl. He put his hands together and said in a dramatic voice, ''Oh, Lord, if this is Your idea of a practical joke, I'm going to become an atheist, I swear.''

Mattie frowned. ''That's not very funny. I'm trying to tell you what you can expect from me, and if that's not what you have in mind, well, then, the whole thing's off.''

Orren shook his head and clapped a hand over his heart. ''Miss Mattie, my love, you've already exceeded my expectations by far. I'd be happy as a hog in slop if you just fed my kids and kept Red from stringing up her sisters. But since you have a system you want to use, you just go right ahead. I'm tickled pink. And if it doesn't work out quite like you have planned, well, then, we'll just make do. That's mostly what we do anyway. Now, I hope you'll go before those four hellions troop back in here and scare the daylights out of you. They can, and they probably will, but I'm hoping you'll at least get the grocery shopping done before you quit. See you in the morning at nine-thirty.'' He grabbed her backpack from the back of the chair and shoved it and her toward the door.

Mattie dragged her feet, but he got her through the door before she could tell him to take his job and shove it. He didn't get it closed, though, because she beat him to the doorknob. She glared up at him from the doorstep and said, ''You are insane, you know.''

He smiled benignly. "And you're going to join me a lot sooner than you realize."

She rolled her eyes at that and pulled the door shut in his face. He couldn't hold back the relief that flooded him, though he knew it was much too early to celebrate. Chances were the poor thing wouldn't last a week, but then again, she just might. She had fortitude, that girl, and she was young enough to take the punishment. Maybe Miss Matilda Kincaid was the answer to his prayers. He hoped so. He very fiercely hoped so.

Chapter Two

Mattie carefully made no mention to her father of the utterly gorgeous Orren Ellis. She said nothing about his well-muscled six-foot frame and carefully kept her thoughts to herself concerning his finely honed, square-jawed face with its sculpted lips and gold-tipped brows. She made no comparisons with bronze and gold and platinum and his slightly curly, sun-streaked hair, which, in her opinion, could use a good cutting. Most of all, she kept secret how shocking were the electric depths of his light blue eyes, fringed lavishly with gold and bronze lashes.

She spoke instead about his four *adorable* children, about Chaz, the little man, and the challenging Jean Marie of the wild red hair, and golden Yancy who adored her big brother, and the picture-perfect little doll baby Candy Sue, whom everyone called Sweetums. They were bright children. They were beautiful children. They were sweet and fun and exciting and just a little needy, and she couldn't wait to get started with them. She just didn't expect to get started with them two hours early the next morning.

Orren was extremely apologetic and even more frantic

than the day before when he called at seven in the morning to ask, to beg, her to come over early. "The mechanic on the early shift has called in sick," he explained, "and I took yesterday off to stay with the kids and interview sitters. I *have* to go in to cover him. Please say you'll come. I don't dare leave these children here alone."

"I'll be there," she said sleepily. "Give me half an hour."

"Thank you, Mattie. Oh, thank you."

Her father was waiting for her when she stepped out of the bathroom. "That call for you?"

"Umm-hmm, Mr. Ellis has been called in early."

"So have you, I take it."

"Right-o."

"Off and running, I guess."

"So it seems. If you don't mind, Dad, I really need to get dressed."

Evans nodded and moved toward the door, but he stopped, pulling the belt of his bathrobe tighter. "I'll make some coffee."

"That'd be great, Dad. Thanks. Uh, you wouldn't mind filling the thermos, would you?"

"Sure. No problem."

She smiled at him as he went out the door, wondering what he'd say if she told him that the thermos of coffee was for Orren, not herself. She pulled on jeans and a T-shirt and got out her sneakers and a pair of thick socks. Something told her she was going to be on her feet a lot today. She yawned and reached for the heavy comb with which to detangle her wet hair.

Her wet hair was hanging down her back when Chaz let her in the door. Orren saw that at a glance, which was all he had time for unless he was going to work without socks. "Mattie, thank God! I'm really sorry about this."

"I brought you something," she said, placing the thermos on the corner of the table while he dug through the mountain of laundry he'd dumped on the couch, Sweetums clinging to his side, her grasping little hands twisting wrinkles in his pale blue uniform shirt. "It isn't a pair of clean socks, is it?"

"Just coffee."

He looked up at that. "Oh, you're good. You're very good."

"Thanks. Need some help?"

"Could you take the baby?" he said, going back to his search. "I know I washed socks. Where are the darned socks?"

She reached for Candy Sue, but the baby was always clingy when she first woke up, and it didn't help that the telephone had jangled her awake hours earlier than usual. She clamped on to him like a leech and shrieked in his ear when Mattie laid hands on her. A crash in the kitchen announced that Mattie's attention was more urgently needed elsewhere.

"Uh-oh." She turned and hurried away in that direction.

"Son," Orren called anxiously, still pawing through the laundry. "Everything okay in there?"

Mattie stuck her head around the short partition wall and said, "A hot waffle iron is melting a hole in the floor vinyl."

"Well, unplug it!"

"I did!"

"Blast!" Orren groaned and staggered as Jean Marie bumped into him, feeling her way along sleepily from behind a curtain of hair.

"I want doughnuts," she said, yawning.

"Not this morning, Red," Orren answered, giving up the search for socks. "See if you can get Sweetums to come to you."

"Let Chaz," Jean Marie grumbled, stumbling toward the kitchen. Yancy screamed from the back bedroom just then, offended at waking up alone, and Candy Sue promptly threw up on his shoulder.

"Aw, baby!" Orren jumped away from the mound of

clean laundry and held Candy out at arm's length. She immediately started to wail. Lord help him! "It's okay, Sweetums. Chaz, bring the antacid! Candy Sue's nervous stomach is acting up again."

He placed Candy Sue in the chair and spread a towel over her in case she threw up again, then ripped his shirt off and threw it on the floor, muttering, "Only clean shirt I had!" He felt like sitting right down and bawling, but that'd make three of them, and he didn't think he could stand it.

Mattie appeared, Chaz on one side, Jean Marie on the other. She was holding the bottle of antacid and a spoon. "Set the water glass down on the end table, Chaz," she directed smoothly, "then take Jean Marie and go quiet Yancy."

Chaz obediently complied. Jean Marie stuck her chin out and opened her mouth. Mattie bent down to her face level, parted the hair curtain with a fingertip and said, "Unless you don't want me to cook breakfast." Jean Marie whirled and stomped after her brother. Mattie straightened and thrust the bottle and spoon at Orren. "You dose the baby," she said, "I'll take care of the shirt. Where's the iron and ironing board?"

He took the medicine, watching as she bent and picked up the soiled shirt, and said, "I don't know. My bedroom, I think."

"I'll find it," she said airily, carrying the shirt away from her.

Orren gratefully sat down next to the baby, spread the towel over the two of them and began the chancy process of coaxing the medication down her. Ten minutes and three attempts later, he judged that he'd gotten enough of the stuff in her to calm her stomach and began rocking her into a better mood. Shortly thereafter she dropped off in his arms. He stood, towel and all, to carry her to his own room, where she *might* be able to sleep undisturbed by the other children. He was surprised—and oddly disturbed—to find

Matilda Kincaid bent over his bed, straightening out his sheets. She certainly looked *adult* from the back. She glanced over her shoulder, something very like censure on her face, but then her expression softened and she stood, turning, to smile down at the frothy-haired angel in his arms. He smiled, too, proud of the little beauty cuddled so trustingly against him.

"She'll never be able to stay asleep in the kids' room," he whispered. "She sleeps most often in here."

Mattie nodded and moved away to retrieve the clean and pressed shirt from the ironing board as he tucked the little one into his bed. She stepped out into the hallway; a second or two later, he joined her, pulling closed the bedroom door. She shook out the uniform shirt and held it up for him, her eyes roaming over his bare chest. Orren resisted the urge to turn his back, and instead dipped one hand into a sleeve hole. She carried the shirt around him and slipped the other sleeve over his arm, settling the shirt over his shoulders.

"I tried to iron it dry, but it's still damp," she said quietly. "At least it didn't stain."

Nodding, he began pushing the buttons through the buttonholes. "That's all right. Thanks."

"No problem," Mattie said, presenting him a pair of matched socks from her belt. "They had dropped down between the bed and the wall."

He clutched them gratefully. "You are a lifesaver!"

"Just part of the service."

"Listen, I'm sorry to run off so quick. I meant to show you around, explain things, but I really don't have the time this morning."

"Oh, don't worry about that," she said cryptically. "I think I can find plenty to keep us busy today."

He was already moving into the living area, only half listening, when he remembered the grocery shopping. He immediately turned back, whipping his wallet from his hip pocket. Emptying it of the last seventy bucks to his name, he thrust it at her apologetically, saying, "Uh, there really isn't anything much here to eat. If you could do the shopping, I'd appreciate it, but this is all I have until the end of the week. We'll, um, discuss a budget later."

"What about your lunch?" she began, but he waved that off, snatched up the thermos and swung out the door. A glance at his watch told him that he just might make it—barely. These days, he reminded himself grimly, *barely* was the best he could hope for.

Mattie shook her head at the boards nailed over the door, the bare gypsum walls and the electrical wires hanging loose. While Candy Sue slept and the other girls watched an educational program on public television, she'd looked over the house in the helpful company of Chaz. It hadn't taken long to get a full picture of Orren Ellis's house, his *unfinished* house. Chaz had told her proudly that his daddy had built the house with his own two hands, and she could understand his pride, but the place was woefully inadequate. For one thing, the kids had been squeezed into a single small room, while this third unfinished bedroom and its badly needed second bath had accumulated debris and gathered dust. Actually, the whole house was a dustbin, not to mention a jumble of chaos. Ah, well, she'd wanted a challenge.

After a scant breakfast of buttered griddle cakes sprinkled with sugar and cinnamon, which the kids wolfed down gleefully, Mattie had found a piece of paper and a pencil and made a list of the family's favorite foods. It wasn't a very extensive list, but it was enough from which to conceive a frugal menu for several days. She then went through the refrigerator and pantry, listing the available supplies and mechanically rearranging the shelves. Everything needed a thorough cleaning, but that would have to wait a bit. First she had a shopping list to make out, carefully estimating the cost of each item and tabulating the whole to be certain that the cost remained safely within the amount allotted.

That proved a simple task compared to getting the children properly dressed for their outing. Their clothing, both clean and dirty, was scattered over the whole house, but eventually she put together outfits for each of them and, by standing over them with an implacable expression, a bar of soap and a tube of toothpaste, saw them dressed and made presentable. It took some time to persuade Jean Marie to brush her hair, but by promising that each of them could choose a favorite food item from the grocery store, she managed even that.

The shopping excursion was a nightmare, with Jean Marie and Yancy playing hide-and-seek in the aisles, Candy Sue begging for everything she laid eyes on, and Chaz desperately badgering, pleading and threatening his sisters while trying all the while to coax Mattie into buying the same items his father always bought. To make matters worse, Candy Sue suddenly developed a pressing need to visit the rest room, while Jean Marie flatly refused to go along. What should have taken an hour at most took more than twice that time, but finally Mattie had the groceries stowed in the trunk, the kids belted in and the little red car on the road to the Ellis house.

By making a game of putting the groceries away, Mattie managed to complete that chore relatively quickly. Then she ferreted out a ragged notebook, sharpened her pencil and set about making her plans. The first order of business, she told an anxious Chaz, was the kitchen, to which he replied, "What's wrong with it?"

So much was wrong with it, to Mattie's mind, that a detailed explanation would take inordinate time and effort, so she settled for pointing out that it was poorly organized and not exactly "sterile." Jean Marie took violent exception to the slightest perceived criticism. Eyes narrowed suspiciously, she declared that the kitchen was forever kept just exactly as their mother had left it. When a gaping Chaz declared aloud that Jean Marie was "cuckoo," she summarily bit him. Luckily, the skin wasn't broken. Mattie marched the little hoyden straight to a corner and stood over her for an entire half hour to keep her there, while Chaz comforted Yancy, who wept loudly on his behalf.

Afterward, Jean Marie disappeared into the bedroom, barricaded the door and shouted insults at Mattie. She was mean and stupid. Her hair was an ugly black color. She was too short and had "baby hands." Chaz helpfully explained that Jean Marie thought "big girls" had long, red fingernails like their mother's. Once the subject of Orren's unfaithful wife had been broached, Mattie found she couldn't quell her curiosity without first asking just a few questions.

Chaz answered each and every one most helpfully. In short order, she found out that Grace Ellis was a tall, blue-eyed beauty with a penchant for tight blue jeans and embarrassingly revealing lingerie. She wore lots of makeup and piled her long blond hair on top of her head. She worried about wrinkles and bragged about her figure. She had shouted at their daddy a lot, said that Candy Sue was "all his fault" and explained repeatedly to her children that she "needed her fun while she could get it." He remembered especially that when she went off with "that man" she'd explained that they were going to get rich on the rodeo circuit and had promised to send them money, but she never had. Chaz divulged, without any prompting, that Orren had gone after Grace upon discovering she had left him, only to return later, all sad, to explain that Mommy was tired of "making do" but sent her love. She wouldn't be coming back, he'd said, except to see them when she could, but she hadn't ever done that, either.

Jean Marie heard it all, having tired of screaming insults and sneaked out of her room. She appeared out of nowhere and immediately denied everything Chaz had said. Their mommy was beautiful and smart and was off getting money. When she came back, they'd all be rich and happy, especially Daddy, who missed her most of all. Mattie carefully schooled her expression and voice, betraying none of the shock and dismay the tale and its refutation had engendered, and calmly suggested that Jean Marie cool her temper unless she wanted to spend another half hour in the corner. With that, she went to make pimento cheese sandwiches and cut up celery, carrots and apples for lunch.

The children, thankfully, were used to entertaining themselves. She had merely to keep an eye and an ear open while they played, occasionally interrupting her work in the kitchen to mediate a minor quarrel or redirect their energies. Even Jean Marie cooperated reluctantly when she promised them a special afternoon snack of cinnamon crisps, which she made from a simple, inexpensive piecrust recipe, cut into strips, and baked in the oven. Candy Sue practically keeled over after the snack, so badly in need of an afternoon nap was she. Yancy was persuaded to join her without much effort, and the two older children went outside to play in the shade of an old live oak on the edge of the front yard within easy sight of the kitchen window. Orren had hung sturdy swings from its thick branches and fashioned a sandbox in an out-of-the-way spot. Mattie dutifully oversaw their play while listening for the younger two and scrubbing down the kitchen cabinets.

All in all, she was well pleased with her day. She had the small kitchen gleaming and the cabinets strictly organized in plenty of time to tell the children a favorite story before stripping the beds and remaking them with clean linens. Then she vacuumed the living room rug, ran a dust cloth over the surface of the battered tables and single lamp and contented herself with straightening up the mess by dispatching the children to other parts of the house with various items in tow, all but Jean Marie who declared that she wasn't "nobody's" slave and locked herself in the bathroom. Mattie let her be until enough of the clutter was removed from the living room to identify it as such, then calmly picked the lock and opened the door.

Jean Marie was lying on the floor beside the tub, her arms flung out dramatically, mouth open, eyes rolled back in her head. An empty, uncapped vitamin bottle that Mattie had noticed in the small wastebasket earlier was clutched in one hand. Mattie smiled to herself, folded her arms, and called out in an unconcerned voice, "Chaz, dear, please bring me a clean spoon so I can poke the handle down Jean Marie's throat and make her throw up all these vitamins the silly girl's taken."

Jean Marie bolted up into a sitting position, her free hand going automatically to her throat as she gagged just at the thought of that spoon handle. Mattie feigned weak relief. "Oh, good. You didn't overdose yourself too badly, after all. Never mind, Chaz. She seems fine now."

In the next instant Jean Marie realized she'd been outfoxed. Sputtering angrily, she threw the vitamin bottle. It bounced harmlessly off the doorjamb and rolled at Mattie's feet. Calmly, Mattie bent and picked it up, then straightened and cocked her head. "Now, young lady," she said, "unless you want me to describe this latest incident to your father, I suggest you improve your behavior." It was then that Jean Marie realized how serious a mistake she'd made. Her daddy wasn't beyond blistering her backside for such a prank. Mutinously, she stuck out her chin. Her eyes filled with tears, but she stubbornly refused to shed them. "You know," Mattie said gently, "we could be friends, you and I, if you'd just let us." Then Mattie left her there and went away.

Orren dragged home utterly exhausted. What a day! A total of three mechanics had called in sick, and he'd been so busy under the hoods of several different cars that he'd hardly had time to answer the telephone. Everything was behind schedule, and he'd endured a rude dressing down from one customer because of it. Tomorrow promised to be a repeat performance, and he was so hungry he could eat lumber. He only hoped Mattie had saved him some supper. She hadn't, but he could hardly grasp what she had done when he walked into his own house and found himself in a strange place.

The kitchen looked like a surgery ward. He'd never seen it shine so. Come to think of it, he couldn't remember the last time he'd seen the tops of the counters, let alone seen them gleam. He'd almost forgotten they were red! Moreover, the table had been properly set with napkins and everything, and the air was filled with the delicious aromas of cooking food. Most astonishing of all, however, was the sight of his children lined up to greet him, heads freshly washed, clothing neat, bodies clean. The babies were ready for bed. Chaz was beaming. Jean Marie showed no visible bruises, though he couldn't imagine anything but brute force producing the astonishing change in her appearance. Her hair had been plaited into a braid! She was wearing shoes *and* socks. Her shorts matched her shirt. He hadn't even known she possessed matching shorts and shirt! Mattie herself looked neat as a pin, even with one of his dish towels tied around her waist like an apron. She quickly whipped it off and suggested that he wash up while she put dinner on the table. Mechanically, he put the thermos he'd brought home on the clean counter and trudged off to do as he was told, marveling at the order in his living room as he did so.

It was almost more than he could fathom, sitting down at the table with his family for a real meal. And what a meal! Boiled beef and noodles in a creamy sauce, green beans, corn and hot bread. When Mattie set a small bowl of pickled beets at his elbow, he could do nothing but gape.

"Chaz said you liked them," she divulged shyly and skittered away.

For the first time he had the presence of mind to look around the table and count the places. Obviously she had been unsure of her welcome at the family table. He twisted in his chair and cleared his throat. When she turned from the sink to look at him, he asked carefully, "Aren't you going to join us?"

Smiling broadly, she plucked another place setting from the cabinet and hurried to squeeze in between Sweetums and Yancy. Once there, however, she dropped her hands to her lap and bowed her head. Uncertain what to make of that, Orren shrugged and reached for the beets, drawing up short when Chaz widened his eyes and frantically shook his head. Thoroughly puzzled, Orren opened his mouth to ask what the dickens was going on, only to be shocked into continued silence by the sight of Chaz folding his hands in an attitude of prayer, his look pleading. Dumbfounded, Orren realized that they were waiting for him to say grace! All but Jean Marie, who tucked her hands into her armpits and narrowed her eyes stubbornly, and Sweetums, who copied Chaz's posture without the least idea why.

Orren cleared his throat, bounced a knee nervously, and took a deep breath, finally blurting, "Thank-you-for-this-food-amen."

Mattie lifted her head, smiling, and began serving dinner.

It beat anything he'd ever seen. Even Jean Marie behaved like a civilized human being and cleaned her plate quickly, despite a pouting silence. Yancy accepted the towel that Mattie tied around her neck bib-fashion, upon realizing that Sweetums was to wear one, also, and ate everything put in front of her, even demanding more. Chaz couldn't say enough good things about Mattie's cooking, and Sweetums managed to giggle charmingly while stuffing her little mouth. After wrapping up the feast with canned pears, they all sat back for a few minutes, replete in a way they never had been before, while Mattie explained about the menu taped to the inside of the pantry door and how she had marked the foodstuffs so they would know what was required for meals and what was available for "unscheduled snacking." She added that she'd tucked the eight dollars left over from the shopping into a jar on the top shelf and suggested that he spend some time with the kids before Candy and Yancy had to be put down to sleep while she cleaned up the kitchen and packed leftovers for his next day's lunch.

Flabbergasted but wise enough to see the benefits of such

a plan, Orren did exactly what she suggested. Only later did he realize that she had slipped away quietly, leaving a note to say she would be in at nine the next morning unless he called to say he wanted her earlier. Bemused, Orren sat down on the couch, pleased that he could, to watch an hour of television with his older children and listen to Chaz glowingly recount their day. Jean Marie was not so thrilled with their new sitter, but her criticism seemed based on nothing more than resentment at being persuaded to behave. In fact, he was a little surprised that her complaints weren't more vehement, but he was too tired to really do anything more than marvel at what one little gal had been able to accomplish in a single day. Later, when he slid between clean, smooth sheets, he decided sleepily that Matilda Kincaid was a sorceress in a teeny-bopper's guise. The next morning, when sitting himself down to enjoy a breakfast of hot muffins, fruit, and—luxury of luxuries—fresh coffee, he silently amended that description to angel, albeit a young one.

Mattie shoved the bed to one side. Jean Marie glared at her from the doorway, arms folded, eyes narrowed, bottom lip jutting out. Mattie sighed. She'd already been told to leave "Mama's bedroom" alone, but once she'd thoroughly cleaned the place, she'd felt an overwhelming urge to make it more attractive. Its bare, bereft nondecor was depressing, and for some reason she wanted to give Orren Ellis reason to be, if not happy, at least pleased. It hadn't taken a lot of effort, really, once she'd been able to get a good look at the room and ferret out some items to use for decoration.

A good washing of the walls had revealed a stuccolike finish of eggshell white. The kids had thought she was nuts when she'd taken brown acrylic paint from one of their battered art sets, thinned it, and used it judiciously to highlight every crack, chip, and mar in the plaster. She'd even gouged a little plaster away in places to heighten the effect and was pleased when the overall look suggested old adobe.

The faded, dirty, entirely too frilly Priscilla curtains were cleaned, dried and put away for the girls to use at a later time, as was the heavy old crocheted bedspread. After washing the windows, she covered them with a pair of golden tan sheers that she'd found in the back of the linen closet in the hallway, then for a valance she tacked up an old horse blanket with which the kids had been playing. An old hand-sewn quilt was thoroughly cleaned and quickly repaired to serve as a bedspread. A headboard for the bed was fashioned from a stack of oak posts discarded as too crooked for use as fencing sometime in the past.

With Chaz's help, Mattie dragged a scarred trunk from the unfinished room, first emptying it of carpentry tools, and placed it at the foot of the bed. Next to it, she arranged a pair of old, nearly rotted cowboy boots and a coiled rope that Chaz insisted his daddy had once used to work the cattle they'd kept on the place. Jean Marie declared this an ugly lie, and Mattie suspected that it had something to do with her mother, but she couldn't imagine what. After receiving specific instructions about what to look for, Chaz unearthed some rusty bits and pieces of bridle, as well as the barrel and stock of a shotgun so ancient it threatened to disintegrate in Mattie's hands as she cleaned it sparingly and hung it on the wall. A battered, almost shapeless, felt cowboy hat came out of a closet somewhere and found a place on the end of a post in the rustic headboard, and a second horse blanket became a bedside rug.

The true challenge in this transformation was presented by the lamp that offered the room's only light source. Pearl white, with gold detailing and a ruffled shade, it was completely out of sync with the new Old West flavor of the room. After much thought and many suggestions from the children, most of them nonsensical but funny, Mattie decided to completely sand the finish of the lamp with sandpaper culled from the unfinished room to give it a rustic look. The shade was another matter. It simply could not be made over to work with the rest of the room, but replacement seemed out of the question—until she came across a tin pail with a hole in the bottom.

Jean Marie volunteered the information that Orren had been furious when Chaz had driven a nail into the pail in a misguided effort to create a shelter for a pet squirrel. The idea had been to attach the pail to a tree in the backyard, but Chaz had been unable to manage that. It seemed that the pail he had chosen was a brand-new one with which Orren had intended to feed the premature, motherless calf he'd secured in the small corral out back. Orren had yelled. Chaz had cried. The squirrel had run away, and eventually the calf had died despite Orren's attempts to save it. The story almost put Mattie off the idea of using the pail, but in the end, it was the only option she could see. She hoped to mitigate the unpleasant memories by having the children draw designs on the side of the pail with crayons, then, using the drawings as patterns, carefully pierce the metal with a hammer and nail. Jean Marie refused to participate, and Mattie wound up having to perform the piercing herself, but once the bail was removed and the hole in the bottom was carefully enlarged, she had herself a suitable, thoroughly unique lamp shade. Jean Marie, however, predicted disaster. Her daddy would hate the dumb old thing, she declared. In fact, he'd hate the whole ugly room.

Mattie was pretty well convinced that Jean Marie was right by the time Orren's truck turned into the driveway. She felt a wave of panic as she heard the engine die away in the carport and the cab door open and close as he got out. Jean Marie waited at the corner of the dinner table, the gleam of retribution in her eyes. When the door opened and Orren pulled himself sluggishly into the house, she launched her offensive.

"She tore up everything!" she declared, pointing an accusing finger at a quaking Mattie. "She took down Mama's pretty curtains and put up a dirty old horse blanket, and she moved everything around, and she punched holes in things! And she got out stuff she wasn't s'posed to, stuff you said we couldn't even get out!"

Orren stood with a hand on the back of his neck, staring at the belligerent child. "What on earth are you talking about, Red?"

Mattie stepped forward, arms rigid at her sides, chin up and confessed. "I redecorated your bedroom."

His mouth fell open, his blue eyes widening. "You *what?*"

"It was presumptuous of me," Mattie admitted, bowing her head. "I don't know quite what came over me except...well, it was depressing, even after I cleaned and reorganized it, and I thought..." She blinked, deciding it was better not to say exactly what she'd thought, that it'd be of benefit to everyone to remove every trace of his ex-wife from the room in which he slept night after night—especially of benefit to her. "If you don't like it," she said with a sigh, "I'll put everything back the way it was. I'll even repaint the walls."

Orren stared at her for what seemed like an eternity, then he rubbed a hand over the top of his head and said tiredly, "Guess we'd better go take a look at it."

Jean Marie ran ahead and smugly threw open the door, while Chaz rushed forward to exclaim that *he* liked the new room, *he* thought it was swell, *he* wished it was *his* room. Orren paused to apologetically pat his son's head and say, "One of these days it will be your room, Chaz, just as soon as I finish the new master bedroom. Promise."

The rather forced smile that Chaz gave his father in return for that promise made it clear that the boy didn't figure it would be kept anytime soon. From the grim expression on Orren's face, Mattie concluded that Chaz was correct; a conclusion which did nothing to calm the butterflies beating madly in her stomach. She held her breath as Orren moved into his room and abruptly stopped, shock registering on his face. Mattie closed her eyes, biting her lower lip to stifle a moan of distress. Suddenly Orren rounded on her.

"I don't believe this!"

Feeling sick, Mattie pressed a hand to her abdomen and quickly said, "I'll put it all back, I swear. I'll do it before I go home tonight."

Orren lifted his hands to his hips. "No way!"

"But—"

Throwing his arms out, he whirled. "This is great! It's wonderful! I can't believe you did this without spending a cent!" Suddenly he whirled back. "You didn't, did you? Spend any money, I mean, because if you bought stuff, it'll have to go back. I can't afford—"

"No!" she interrupted. "I didn't buy a thing! I just sort of...rearranged stuff."

He grinned and pivoted to take another look. "This is amazing. You're a genius, Mattie, I swear you are! Man, I'm sure glad I didn't throw any of this stuff away. I nearly stomped that pail there, and I can't tell you how many times I meant to burn those old crooked fence posts!"

"I he'ped!" Yancy said around the thumb in her mouth.

"Me, too!" Chaz admitted proudly.

"They all did," Mattie said, tossing a glance in Jean Marie's direction.

Jean Marie clamped her jaw and glared at her, tears gathering in her eyes. She advanced on her father. "You don't like all this junk, do you?"

Orren smiled, completely missing the import of the question. "I like it real fine, Red. Y'all did a good job."

"But what about Mama's curtains?" she cried.

Orren turned a confused face at Mattie. "I put them away," she said softly. "I thought if...*when* the girls get a room of their own, they might like to use them in there."

"Now that's a good idea," Orren said a bit too heartily, finally having divined the problem. "You'll like that, won't you, Red? Maybe we can put up one of those borders you see in all the stores these days, too."

"And we can dye the curtains and bedspread to match," Mattie offered helpfully. "With some pretty throw pillows and a nice scarf or two we could—"

Crying out in frustration and rage, Jean Marie tore from the room and out of the house. Sighing, Orren bowed his head in defeat.

"I'm so sorry," Mattie said. "I didn't realize how sensitive she is about her mother's things. I shouldn't have made any changes without consulting you first, either. Maybe we should put everything back."

Orren shook his head. "Mattie, I owe you a debt of gratitude. You read me just right, figuring what I'd like and all, and you did a fine job in here. I never imagined what all you could do for us when I hired you! Makes me wish I could keep you on past the end of summer, but since everybody will be going back to school, you included.... Well, never mind that. The thing is, I like this room a whole lot better now than I ever did before, and Red has to accept the fact someday that her mother isn't ever coming back. I wish I knew what to say to her to make her understand. Lord knows I've tried, and I reckon I'll just have to keep on trying. But you don't owe anybody any apologies. Now, if it's all right with you, I'll wash up and go talk to her while you get dinner on the table. My belly's beating against my backbone, I'm so hungry, and whatever you've cooked up in there sure smells good."

Mattie smiled and nodded. "All right. It won't take long. The meat loaf's done, and the macaroni's almost ready."

Orren licked his lips and made hungry noises while she turned away and headed for the kitchen. He slipped out the door a few minutes later, and soon after that returned with a pouty Jean Marie in tow. Her eyes and nose were red from crying, and her attitude had not noticeably improved, but she said nothing as she sullenly ate her dinner, then disappeared into the back of the house.

Mattie made short work of the post-dinner cleanup, while Orren spent time with the youngest two girls before putting them down for the night. When she gathered her things to make her usual low-key departure, however, Orren appeared to thank her once again for all she'd done.

"You are one talented young lady," he said. "I don't know anyone your age anywhere who could do what you've done. One of these days you'll make a fine wife and mother."

He hadn't the least idea how dismaying his words were to Mattie. None of her efforts, she realized, had made him see her as the adult she was inside, if not outside. Perhaps it was time for another sort of transformation, this time of herself.

Chapter Three

It was just a sundress, and that's exactly what Mattie told her father, patiently, unconcernedly, determinedly. He didn't buy a syllable of it.

"That thing's indecent!" he exclaimed, walking a circle around her, the better to become outraged by the strapless bandeau top and the short slit skirt that exposed the matching short-shorts. "You've worn bathing suits less revealing than that!"

"And will again," she assured him nonchalantly. "In fact, if you prefer, I could wear one today and save myself the same hassle."

"What's that supposed to mean?"

She sighed and flipped the long tail of her hair over her shoulder. "We're going to lie out in the sun today," she explained, delivering the well-thought-out excuse. "The kids should start swimming lessons soon, and I want us all to get a little sun first. I *don't* want to have to change my clothes twice to manage it."

Evans scowled but couldn't argue with her logic. Amy stepped into the fray, lifting a loving hand to her husband's shoulder, sending a knowing look to Mattie. "Honestly, Evans, you sound like the father of a twelve-year-old instead of a twenty-year-old."

"She's *not* twenty!"

"She's closer to twenty than nineteen."

"That dress would be indecent at fifty!"

Amy smirked. "Now I agree with you there, unless, of course, the fifty-year-old should have a body like a twenty-year-old. Give over, Dad. Your little girl is all grown up and has a perfect right to wear anything she wants."

"Oh, and I have no right to voice my opinion, I suppose," Evans sulked.

"You have as much right to voice your opinion, Daddy, as I have to ignore it," Mattie said blithely, and with that she went up on tiptoe to kiss his cheek. "See you tonight. Have a good day. Bye, Amy." Trilling her fingers at her stepmother, she sauntered down the hall, ignoring the heatedly whispered conversation taking place behind her. Poor Daddy. How upset he would be if he knew upon what campaign she had just embarked!

Orren frowned at the Mattie who stood before him, busily pinning up her hair. If she was not careful that so-called dress was going to show more than it already did, and it showed quite enough already—more than enough. The sight of all that pale golden skin made him decidedly nervous. His hands were shaking, for pity's sake! Not that he found her attractive exactly, not in the same way as he'd found Gracie attractive. Heavens, no. Gracie was sexy, blatantly so, almost embarrassingly so. She had often referred to herself as a "hot property," and no one had ever argued with the assessment. Gracie breathed heavy sexuality and had from a very early age. He imagined she'd appeared more worldly and womanly at twelve than Matilda Kincaid did at twenty. There was something *innocent* about Mattie, something *wholesome.* Actually, coupled with her very sleek, almost exotic beauty, it was pretty heady stuff. But it just wasn't the kind of thing that really attracted him. Not really, *really* attracted him, anyway. Of course not. She was much too young, just a girl. He scraped his fingers through his hair, just to have something to do with his hands, and cleared his throat.

"So you think I should let the kids take swimming lessons," he said, as much to call himself back to the subject at hand as to let her know that he'd been listening.

She snatched a hairpin from her mouth and stabbed it into the twist of hair atop her head. "Absolutely. They're never too young to learn something so important."

"I agree," he said, embarrassed and irritated, "but there's one little problem."

"Oh? And what is that?"

He ground his teeth together. "I can't afford swimming lessons."

She blinked at him as if that idea hadn't occurred to her at all. "It doesn't cost anything. At least, no more than you're paying me now."

It was his turn to blink. "You mean, *you* are going to teach them?"

"Of course. I have certification from California. I used to live there, you know."

Actually, he hadn't known, but he nodded, anyway. It was so typically Mattie. Of course she'd teach them herself! He should have expected that by now. Was there anything she couldn't do? He felt a step behind suddenly, but he was becoming accustomed to that. Thinking rather desperately, he came up with another question. "Where were you thinking of doing it?"

"Teaching them, you mean?"

"That's right."

She shrugged. "I have a friend with a backyard pool. I thought we'd start there."

He cocked his head. "What friend would that be?" *Male or female?* he wondered specifically.

"Terri Whiteside."

His stomach dropped. Male or female? he asked himself again, then shook his head over the stupidity of it. What was it to him? Nothing! Except, of course, as it pertained to his children. He wouldn't want anything untoward to take place in front of them. If Mattie had a boyfriend—and of course she did!—he had better make sure that she understood what type of behavior he expected from her. He opened his mouth to speak, but she beat him to it.

"Now, don't take that attitude," she scolded gently. "We won't let anything happen to them. Terri will be there with us, of course, and she's a very good swimmer herself. We'll be very careful, I promise."

She. She's a very good swimmer. The level of relief he felt was absurd in the extreme. But then, his children were very precious to him. He had a perfect right to be concerned about who and what they were exposed to. And where they were taken, for that matter. He cleared his throat again, striving for the perfect fatherly tone. "Where, um, exactly does this Terri Whiteside live?"

She gave him an address, which he committed to memory. It was a good part of town, not the country club section exactly but solidly middle class. "I thought we'd start next week, if that's all right with you."

He nodded, still feeling as if he'd been given a reprieve of some sort. "Fine. Uh, if you're sure that it's all right with her parents."

She gave him a quizzical look. "Her parents?" Suddenly a smile quirked at one corner of her mouth. "Oh." She brought her hands to her hips in what was a patently Mattie gesture. "You thought she lives with her parents. Actually, she is checking with her roommates, but I don't expect any problems. They both work days. Terri works nights, see, so she's the only one there during the daytime."

"Roommates," he muttered, feeling decidedly embarrassed. Why hadn't he thought of that?

She smiled knowingly. "Yeah. Originally, I was supposed to be there with them, but in the end I couldn't see any reason to pay rent when I didn't have to." The smile became a grin. "Especially since I have complete access to the pool anytime I want."

Orren felt the beginning of a burn at the base of his throat. "I see. Well, it's all right with me if it's all right with...everyone else. Uh, the swimming lessons, I mean."

She lifted her hands in a gesture of completion. "Great! I brought some sunscreen so we can all lie out in the sun a little while today. I don't like to expose myself all at once. It's safer to do it gradually."

Her choice of words brought to mind a picture that had to be hastily erased. Mattie. Exposed. He gulped. "Uh, you ought to be able to find bathing suits for everyone around here."

"I already have, but we won't need them just yet."

"I see. All right. Well—" he shifted his weight "—I'd better go."

"Oh, wait just a second." She suddenly dipped two fingers into the center of her bodice and extracted a folded slip of paper, which she extended unceremoniously. "I recently had my cellular phone reactivated in this area, and I thought you ought to have the number."

Orren tried to ignore where that bit of paper had come from and the slight warmth that clung to it, but his hands were trembling again when he unfolded it, glanced at the number scribbled inside, then tucked it safely into a front pocket of his navy blue uniform pants. "Th-thanks." He headed for the door, anxious to get out of there, to think of something else besides the shadowed cleavage between those high, firm breasts.

"Orren," she called lightly after him.

He paused and glanced back over his shoulder. Why did he feel as if she were holding a gun to his back? "Yes?"

"Will you be home at your usual time this evening?"

He shook his head, then nodded, both an effort to clear the cobwebs from his brain rather than in answer to her question. "Uh, actually I ought to be a little early. We have a fairly light afternoon scheduled."

She beamed at him. "Great! I'll be sure to have dinner ready early. Have a good day."

He was nodding when he went through the door, feeling for all the world as if he'd just escaped with his life. What was going on here? She was the baby-sitter, for pity's sake, a *teenager.* Wildly, he wondered if she realized how like a wife she had sounded just then and decided that she probably did not. Never mind the strapless getup, she was still just a girl. Well, if not a girl, exactly, then still far too young to be thinking of him as anything other than her employer.

He probably seemed like an old man to her, divorced and with four kids and all. He certainly felt like an old man sometimes, though lately, since Mattie had come into their lives, things had been easier. He'd been getting more rest and had less to worry him. The regular meals didn't hurt, either. The kids seemed satisfied, even Jean Marie, who never had anything kind to say about Mattie. Somehow, the money even seemed to go farther. Come to think of it, he hadn't ever had it as easy as he did just now. Heaven knew that Gracie was no housekeeper and not much of a cook, either. But this was a temporary situation at best. He had to remember that.

Summer would end, and the kids and Mattie would all go back to school. He'd be scrambling for after-school care again, and paying through the nose for it while trying to do everything on his own that Mattie was doing for them now. Mattie would be off at college hitting the books and doing all the things that college kids enjoyed, while he'd be back to the same old grind. It made him tired just to think of it. No wonder he was beginning to imagine Mattie as more than a very intelligent, organized, talented *teenage* baby-sitter.

Suddenly he had it all figured out. And it was perfectly natural! He wasn't losing his mind. He wasn't responding inappropriately to a girl much too young for him. He was just understandably dreading how it would be when this nice little interlude was over. And maybe he was grateful, too. That would be perfectly normal. Now all he had to do was remember what was going on here, then just to enjoy these moments of peace in the chaos that was his life—and rest up for what was sure to come around again. After Mattie. Yes, all he had to do was to remember what was coming after Matilda Kincaid.

Mattie smiled and quickly bowed her head, pretending not to notice as Orren lightly whacked the back of Jean Marie's head before bowing his own. Jean Marie glared belligerently, tucked her hands into her armpits and only then bowed her head. She did not close her eyes as her father prayed, but she didn't bump the table with her legs or scatter the flatware beside her plate with her elbow this time. She was slowly getting better at accepting the changes around her—and Orren was getting better with his prayers. Mattie's heart turned over in her chest as he thanked God for her and all she'd done for them. After the Amen, she lifted her head and smiled at him.

"That was very sweet of you, but I just do what you pay me to do."

"Oh, you do more than that," he said, passing her a bowl of creamed potatoes. "Just look at the nice new bedroom I have."

"Dad?" Chaz said from the end of the table. "When can I have my own room?"

It had escaped no one's attention that Chaz deeply coveted the very masculine new decor of his father's room, a room that had evidently been meant to be his as soon as his father completed the new master bedroom he'd been building when his mother had left them. Orren lowered his hands to the table and glanced in Mattie's direction before turning his attention to his son. "I've been thinking about that, son," he said carefully, and then turned his attention back to Mattie. "The thing is, I'll be needing to take some work on the side to pay for building supplies so I can finish the room. Which means I'll be needing you to stay with the kids a little more."

She twirled her fork in her potatoes and said lightly. "That's fine."

"I—I can't pay you a lot extra," he went on nervously.

"We'll work something out," she told him smoothly.

He nodded and dropped his gaze to his plate. Mattie swept her hair away from her face, twisted it and pulled it all over one shoulder, effectively baring her back, thanks to the clinging halter-top bathing suit that she wore beneath her jeans. Just as she'd expected—and hoped—Orren shot a reluctant glance over her. He didn't want to notice, but he did. Carefully concealing her smile, she asked, "How long do you think it will take to finish the room?"

He scowled, but she knew that look wasn't for her. "Probably all summer," he said gloomily, and Chaz groaned aloud. Jean Marie stuck out her tongue at him. Mattie pressed on determinedly.

"I've given this some thought, too," she said, "and I was wondering why we couldn't just move some things out of the way and sort of wall in one corner with curtains and put a bed for Chaz in there. That way, everyone would have some privacy, and when you get the room finished, or nearly so, you and Chaz could change places."

"That's not a bad idea," he said, lifting his eyebrows at Chaz. Chaz nodded eagerly. Only Jean Marie objected.

"No! That's not fair! How come Chaz gets his own room, and I don't?"

"But there will be one less in your room," Mattie pointed out patiently.

Jean Marie slapped the tabletop with one palm, tears springing to her eyes. "I want my own room, too!"

"Jean Marie," Orren began sternly, "I can't afford to build you your own room. Chaz is a boy. He shouldn't have to share with a bunch of girls."

"Then why do *I* have to share? It's not fair!"

Orren sighed. "Listen, Red, I'd build you your own room if I could, but—"

"You hate me!" she cried, leaping to her feet. "You just hate me! Everyone hates me!" With that she whirled and ran from the room.

Orren was up and after her in a heartbeat. "No one hates you, Red! Come back here!"

In a few moments a melodramatically heartrending scream came from the back of the house. Mattie shook her head as Chaz rolled his eyes, but Candy Sue bought it, her little chin wobbling as she screwed up her eyes and burst into sobs. Yancy, of the ever ready waterworks, was right behind her. Mattie got up from her chair, going around to stand between them and offer each a comforting arm. "It's all right," she crooned. "You know Daddy wouldn't hurt Jean Marie. She's just upset, and she's always loud when she's upset. Isn't she, Chaz?"

"I'll say! Especially when she doesn't get her own way. She's just jealous 'cause I'm finally gonna get my own room!"

Yancy suddenly realized what this meant, too. Her eyes growing enormous, she looked at Chaz, yanked her thumb from her mouth and exclaimed, "I stay with you, Chaz!"

Chaz smacked himself in the middle of the forehead, exclaiming, "You can't, Yancy! It wouldn't be my own room then!"

Yancy began to cry in earnest, as if Chaz was truly abandoning her by moving into his own room. Candy Sue was momentarily intrigued by the spectacle Yancy was making and forgot to cry for a while, giving Mattie time to comfort Yancy alone.

"There now, sweetheart, it's all right. Chaz will be just next door, and I tell you what we'll do, we'll fix up your room real pretty. We'll...I know, we'll fix up one corner or one wall for each of you. How would that be? You'll get your very own wall!"

"You can have the wall closest to my room," Chaz suggested helpfully.

Yancy's tears dried instantly. She looked Mattie straight in the eye and said, "I want my wall yellow."

Mattie laughed and hugged her, and suddenly they were all laughing. Orren came back to the table just then, his scowl lightening some at their obvious mirth. "What's so funny?" he asked, seating himself.

Candy Sue endeavored to make the explanation—and herself the center of attention. Leaning forward at the waist she announced solemnly, "Yancy gets wellow wall."

Orren smiled. "What?"

Yancy waded in with her own explanation. "I want my wall in the girls' room to be yellow."

"Your wall in the girls' room?" Orren echoed, looking to Mattie for explanation.

"Well, I thought each of the girls could have her own wall in *their* room, and Yancy wants her wall to be yellow."

Orren's mouth wiggled. "Yellow?"

"Wellow!" Candy Sue confirmed, and everyone laughed again, Orren included.

He picked up his fork. "I suppose we could afford a little paint." Mattie smiled at him gratefully. "What about you, Sweetums? What color do you want your wall?"

Candy Sue stared at her father as if she didn't understand a word he'd just said. Then suddenly she shouted, "Pink!" She looked at each of her stunned audience in turn, chanting, "Pink, pink, pink!" She started clapping her hands. "Pink, pink, pink!"

Yancy was the first to recover. Picking up the chant, she began to clap her hands, too. "Pink, pink, pink!" Then she abruptly switched to "Yellow, yellow, yellow!"

Chaz slapped both hands over his face, shaking his head at the cacophony. Orren chuckled and waved his fork and knife for silence. "Okay, okay. We've got pink and yellow. That's two walls."

Sudden inspiration hit Mattie. "Two of four," she said, and Orren seemed to instantly pick up on her train of thought.

"Three girls, four walls. What are we going to do with the fourth wall? Maybe it ought to go to the oldest?" He put his fork and knife down and got up again. "I'll be right back."

Mattie hugged each of the girls and Chaz in turn before returning to her own chair. She had managed to get everyone's plate filled except the two absentees by the time they returned. Jean Marie's eyes were red from crying, but she had allowed herself to be mollified with the offer of two walls of her own to each of the other girl's one each. Orren sent Mattie a grateful look, then settled into his chair and began filling Jean Marie's plate for her. Jean Marie sat silently until he'd finished with her plate and began to work on his own. Then she picked up her fork, slid it into a pile of green beans and looked at Mattie.

"I want my walls to be purple," she said in a voice husky with the aftermath of tears. "Light purple."

Mattie nodded in understanding and began to eat, her mind busy with ways to dress up a single room in three different colors for three little girls whose mother should have been there to oversee. She knew she'd have to use the things she'd taken from Orren's bedroom, and yet somehow she had to make them new again, make them special to Jean Marie as her own, not just her absent mother's. She decided to ask Orren if she could dye the curtains and bedspread, and that brought to mind some of her own things that she'd once dyed—bright yellow, as it happened. Suddenly her vision broadened and the room began to take shape before her mind's eye. She decided to say nothing to Orren about her plans for the room, beyond asking his permission to dye the necessary curtains and bedspread. She wanted to surprise him with what she could do, given the chance. He was starting to take notice, and she meant to fix his interest if at all possible. He needed her. They all needed her. And she needed them. They were exactly what she needed, Orren especially.

She thought about how hard he worked, how hard he tried to do well by his children, how selflessly he sacrificed for them. She thought of his pride in Chaz and his patience with Jean Marie, the respect he showed Yancy, the wistfulness with which he indulged his little Sweetums. He never spoke of his ex-wife, never complained about his lot in life even though he sometimes looked so tired when he came home at night that she wanted to cry for him. Instead he kept his head down and his nose to the grindstone, allowing his life and world to be defined by his children and their needs. Well, what about his needs? Someone ought to think of that. She'd had a little taste of it, and she knew that she wanted to be the one to think of him, to fill his needs. Something inside her recognized that this was what she was all about. She was meant for this. She was good at it. She would be better still. Oh, yes, Orren Ellis didn't know it yet, but her very greatest talent was going to be loving him.

Mattie straightened and stretched her aching back. Moving around all that junk in Chaz's new "room" the day before had taken a definite toll on her, but it had been worth it. They'd tacked up some colorful, if rather worn, quilts to cover the bare walls and rigged up a room divider with old curtain rods, a pole, a little baling wire, and a combination of blankets and frayed drapes. It was makeshift at best, but once his bed was set up inside the cozy cubicle, established, Chaz was in seventh heaven. He moved in his belongings with the proprietary air of a new home owner, crawling on his belly to stash his precious stuff beneath the bed, setting up his rickety bedside table and lamp with complete self-assurance, pinning posters to the fabric walls, arranging with scientific precision the plastic milk crates that served as his dresser and closet. Jean Marie turned up her nose at the tentlike structure that had become his very own room, but Chaz couldn't be bothered with petty jealousy. He was out on his own at last, the single male, aloof from the pack.

The girls, meanwhile, were discovering the joys of single-sex habitation. They were free to gather ruffles and tie bows at their leisure. The dolls came out, along with all their clothes and accessories. Cheap costume jewelry in pastel shades appeared around their necks. An inordinate amount of hairbrushing began. Mattie was bemused by the helpful eagerness with which it was all packed away again and shoved aside so the painting could begin.

Orren helped with that part of it. Mattie and the girls picked up paint samples from the local discount store and brought them home, where they pored over them endlessly before marking their choices. Orren stopped by the store on his way home from work the next evening and picked up the paint and necessary supplies. The next day was Sunday, his day off, and he used it to tape off the woodwork, light fixtures and ceiling and begin the painting. He finished up on Monday, removed the masking tape, made any necessary touch-ups and put away his materials. With all the furnishings piled beneath plastic in the center of the floor and the four walls painted pastel shades of lilac, rose pink and buttercup yellow, the room looked decidedly odd, but Mattie had plans.

On Tuesday, she brought with her a thin sheet of plastic, a ruler, a special knife with a razor-thin blade, and a coloring book of flowers. After relatively little discussion, the girls chose a tulip from the book of flowers. Using a pencil, Mattie carefully measured the flower and the sheet of plastic, calculated how many copies of the flower could be cut into the plastic, and with a pencil outlined the flower on the plastic sheet. After meticulously cutting out the shapes of the flower with the special knife, she had a stencil. Using a sponge and the same paint Orren had used on the walls, she carefully stenciled pink and yellow tulips on the lilac walls and lilac tulips on the pink and yellow walls. Then, using ink markers from the kids' own art supplies, she carefully drew bows on each tulip stem and allowed the girls to color them in with crayons. The result was very "little girl" and quite delightful. The girls were clearly entranced.

But Mattie was nowhere near finished. After arranging the furniture so that the correct bed rested against the correct wall, mismatched twin beds for Jean Marie and Yancy and a crib, still, for Candy Sue, Mattie set about making them "fit." Every piece was banged up and scraped, but they were solid and serviceable. Borrowing a little sandpaper from Chaz's temporary room, Mattie lightly went over each piece, then painted and detailed the pieces with the same paint they'd used for everything else. She wound up with a yellow spindle bed trimmed in pink and lilac, a lilac four-poster trimmed in yellow and pink, and a pink crib trimmed in lilac and yellow. Suddenly the room was beginning to really pull together. Even Jean Marie was almost painfully excited.

The problem came the next day with the curtains. The curtains that Mattie had taken from Orren's room simply did not fit the window in the girls' room. Yet, she had promised Jean Marie that they would use them. Orren had given her permission to dye anything she wanted to dye and four bucks to do it with. The washing machine did the hardest part, but the curtains had to be put through twice before they approximated the color of the bedspread. They were all a bit darker than the lilac on the walls, but Mattie judged it the best they could do, and Jean Marie was, for once, completely tractable. Unfortunately the curtains were just completely wrong for the window.

After much trial and error, Mattie loaded the kids in the car and drove them to her father's house. They were clearly intrigued by the house where Mattie lived and clearly intriguing to Mattie's stepmother, Amy. They spent more time in the kitchen chatting with Amy and ruining their lunch with thick slices of angel food cake garnished with canned peaches than helping Mattie go through the carefully packed boxes of old curtains and linens in the attic.

Mattie found what she needed, anyway, and loaded her treasures in the trunk of the car before buckling her wards into their seat belts.

Back at the Ellis house, Mattie reshaped curtain rods, washed and pressed curtains and bedspreads and table covers, drove nails and twisted in screws, glued, taped, pinned, stapled, and thumbtacked until her hands were sore and finally stood back to apprise her efforts. It was brilliant, if she did say so herself. Jean Marie's newly dyed lilac curtains, which had once belonged to her idolized mother, now draped the head of her bed and were tied back and pinned to the wall, creating what Jean Marie declared a "princess look." Tiers of ruffled yellow café curtains covered the window. A flowered set of queen-size sheets became bedspread, pillow shams, lamp shade and table cover for Yancy's bed and tiny side table. A fuzzy pink twin-size blanket performed a similar service for Candy Sue's crib, which Mattie lowered as much as possible before letting down the side so that Candy Sue was able to climb in and out of her bed safely all by herself. A white bath mat became a suitable rug when pierced at measured intervals and scraps of cloth from the bed sheets and yellow, pink and lilac ribbons were threaded through the holes and tied like fringe. With a number of pretty pictures, from an oversize book of fairy tales that had come apart, tacked to the walls, some throw pillows scattered around, and their toys and clothing organized and stowed away in the closet and boxes under their beds, the room looked as fine as any Mattie had ever seen.

The girls were so thrilled that they clapped their hands, sang and danced around the room before throwing themselves at Mattie in exuberant joy. Even Jean Marie forgot her resentment long enough to join in covering Mattie's face with kisses before crowing to anyone who would listen that her "princess" bed was the best of everything in the room. Chaz tried to dismiss it all as useless girl stuff, but he kept laughing and clapping with the rest of them.

Mattie could hardly wait for Orren to come home and see what wonders she had wrought, not only with the room but with his daughter. Tired as she was, she couldn't help humming as she bathed the girls and then prepared a simple dinner of chili pie and salad. Chaz and Jean Marie set the table by themselves as the two younger girls were out of it. Candy Sue was practically asleep on her feet, having missed her usual afternoon nap, and Yancy simply couldn't tear herself away from her yellow wall. She lay across her bed, her legs plastered to the wall, talking to her doll in whispers as her stockinged feet danced to a tune only they could hear.

When Mattie heard the sound of Orren's truck, she left dinner on the stove and in the refrigerator, then ushered the children into a weary but happy line beside the dining table. Beside herself with anticipation, she stood with them, a great big smile on her face. Orren opened the door and stepped up into the kitchen, his steps dragging from tiredness. He shot them a smile and set his lunch kit on the counter.

"What's this? I haven't had a welcoming committee since the first day Mattie came."

Mattie rocked up on her tiptoes. "We have something to show you."

He didn't have to think very hard to realize what it must be. "Can't wait until after dinner, huh? Gotta show off the room right now?"

"*Now,* Daddy," Jean Marie insisted, stepping forward to catch his hand while Yancy hopped in place and clapped her hands.

"Wait till you see my yellow wall!"

"My pink one!" Candy Sue yelled, popping her thumb from her mouth.

"It's all girlie!" Chaz exclaimed, but his grin belied the scorn in his tone.

"I've got a princess bed!" Jean Marie was saying, tugging him along. They all turned and hurried through the living room along the hallway past the bath and to the door of the "new" room. Mattie's hand went to the doorknob; she paused a moment to heighten the drama, then flung open the door. The girls burst into the room, laughing and screaming with anticipated delight. Chaz pushed Orren inside and followed after him, leaving Mattie to bring up the rear and stand, with arms folded, against the door frame.

Orren stopped in the middle of the floor and looked down at the rug on which he stood, stepped back hastily and turned his gaze slowly around the room. His jaw slowly dropped as he made the first circle, then clamped shut as he made the next. Finally he turned his gaze on Mattie. Only then did she realize that he was not exactly pleased.

"What's wrong?" she asked, straightening away from the door casing.

"What's wrong?" he demanded. "What are you trying to do, break me?"

"No!"

"This must've cost a fortune!" Orren insisted, color rising in his face.

"But it didn't! I didn't spend any extra, I swear."

"Then where did this all come from?" He gestured around him angrily, the children shrinking back in surprise.

"Most of it was already here," Mattie said, determined to be reasonable. "Some of it is...*was* mine. I brought it over from my house."

"And Mattie's stepmother gave us cake and peaches!" Chaz put in helpfully.

The color abruptly drained from Orren's face. He glared at Mattie, a vein pulsing in the hollow of his temple. "Get it out of here," he said. "Take it all back."

Predictably, Jean Marie stepped forward and objected. "No! You can't do that! We want it! It's our special room now!"

"We don't take charity!" Orren thundered, but his gaze was fixed on Mattie.

Glancing reassuringly at the children, Mattie opened her

mouth to explain, but he suddenly pushed past her and was gone. Yancy began to wail. Jean Marie threw herself face-down on her "princess" bed and began to sob. Candy Sue collapsed upon the floor and followed suit, while Chaz moved anxiously from Yancy to Candy Sue trying to calm and quiet them. Mattie looked around her at the fine room and the weeping children and felt her own expectations die. Her great accomplishment, it seemed, was a dismal failure.

Chapter Four

Orren slammed out of the house, stomped down the two steps to the floor of the carport and yanked open the pickup truck door, where he stopped, realizing only then that he didn't have anywhere to go. Growling a favorite swearword around the shop, he slammed the door shut again and stalked over to the wall of storage units standing mere feet from the truck bumper. Fishing a key ring from his pocket, he selected the correct key and inserted it into the padlock that protected his tools. Opening the telescoping shelves wide, he selected a wrench, pulled a faded red shop rag from a bag on a hook and began to polish the already gleaming steel. Finding nothing to worry him, he hung up the wrench and selected another. He always kept his tools clean and properly stored. They were essential to his livelihood and too expensive to treat carelessly. And there was a certain peace to be found in the mindless action necessary to keep them well oiled and rust free.

As he rubbed a drop of clear oil into the adjustment mechanism, he blanked his mind to what had just taken place inside the house. He didn't want to think about the amazing transformation Mattie had wrought in his daughters' bedroom or how totally inadequate she had made him feel at the moment of revelation. All he'd done was paint four walls three different colors as he was told, and suddenly his house looked like a magazine layout. But even she couldn't make such changes with the wave of magic wand. She had to go out begging trappings from her father's house! He didn't know quite why that rankled him so.

Maybe it had to do with the fact that he'd spoken to Evans Kincaid father-to-father that day on the telephone. Kincaid had sounded like a strong, conscientious father, the sort Orren wanted to be himself, the sort he tried to be. Come to think about it, he wanted his daughters to be like Mattie: sweet, wholesome, self-possessed, geniuses. Dang, she was smart! He would never have dreamed of doing up that room like she had. She could make a dollar go around the block twice while everyone else was just trying to stretch one to the end of the drive. If only she hadn't taken things from Evans Kincaid's house to fix up his, he could be happy for his girls. But he didn't want them feeling like charity cases! One thing they had never done was accept charity, and they weren't going to start now!

The sound of the door to the house opening set his teeth on edge, but he did his best to ignore it. He was hoping it was Chaz. Oh, how he was hoping those light, uncertain footsteps belonged to Chaz!

"Orren?"

Mattie's voice shivered over him. Steeling himself, he hung up the wrench, wiped his hands on the rag, closed the swinging shelves and snapped the padlock into place. He stuffed the rag into his pants pocket and finally turned. "I meant it. The Ellis family doesn't take charity. Take it all back home."

She folded her arms and said flatly, "No."

He was not a short-tempered man, but his temper ignited then. "Damn it, Mattie, do as I tell you! I don't want that stuff in my house! You had no right to bring it here to begin with!''

''You told me I could redecorate the girls' room.''

''I didn't think you were going to go out and strip your father's house in order to do it!''

She rolled her eyes. ''Don't be stupid! Those things came out of the attic. They were destined for a garage sale, at best!''

''All right, if you won't take them back, then I'll have to buy them from you.'' He whipped out his wallet. ''How much?''

Mattie stepped back, her mouth falling open. ''How dare you? That's the most insulting thing you've ever—''

''Insulting! Is it insulting to want to pay your own way? Is it insulting to want to do for your children yourself?''

''You *are* doing for you children, Orren. You knock yourself out for your children. Don't you think I see that?''

''I don't know what you see, Mattie! Apparently, whatever it is, you don't like it much, because you seem determined to change it!''

''That's not true! I just want to help.'' She stepped close, hands raised beseechingly, emerald eyes glowing. ''You work so hard, Orren. Sometimes when you come in you look so tired I want to cry for you. I just want to make the place nice—for you and the kids.''

It was the kind of thing a wife might have said to her husband to justify blowing big bucks on something for the house, and it shook him right down to the soles of his feet. She was the baby-sitter, for pity's sake, not his spouse! ''I hired you to watch my kids and fix their meals, not to turn my house upside down!'' he pointed out heatedly. ''I don't even recognize the place anymore!''

She looked as if he'd hit her, her emerald eyes wide and shimmering. ''I—I see. I'm sorry. I didn't realize I'd overstepped. I'll…I'll just go now. Dinner's on—'' she gulped, and he realized belatedly that she was fighting back tears ''—the s-stove!'' She whirled away and made for the steps.

In less time than it took to snap his fingers, the anger drained away and regret poured in. Suddenly, he felt like the world's worst ogre. "Mattie, stop!"

She did just as she was told, freezing in place.

"I didn't mean to make you cry," he told her, morosely confused himself.

"I understand," she said, her voice thick with tears. "My fault. I tend to…t-take over." She sniffed and swiped at her eyes, saying softly, "It's all right."

Now he *really* felt low. "No, it's not. You didn't mean any harm."

She whirled back to him, fresh tears brimming in her eyes. "I really didn't, Orren, I swear! I thought it would make the girls happy and give Chaz a place of his own and take the heat for it off you! I only wanted—" Her chin wobbled, and his heart turned over.

"I know, I know," he crooned, stepping up close and wrapping an arm around her shoulders, much as he would one of the kids. "It's all right. You were trying to help." He brushed a tendril of dark, silky hair off her face. Awareness shivered up his spine. She was not, after all, a child, no matter how determined he might be to think of her as one. He thought he might be… No, he was definitely in trouble.

She turned her face up, and her small, strong hand cupped the knob of his shoulder. "Please don't be angry with me," she whispered, her full, pink lips forming each word perfectly.

He felt his hand warming the back of her neck and wondered how it had gotten there; then he forgot about it as his gaze targeted the luscious lips moving closer to his own. He dropped his eyelids—terrified by what he knew was coming and felt powerless to prevent—just as his mouth covered hers. She sucked in a quick breath through her nostrils and went absolutely still, as if stunned or dismayed by the turn of events. But then her hand slid upward into his hair at the back of his head, her mouth parting beneath his.

Heat exploded in his torso and radiated outward, warming his bones and sinews and finally popping through his skin in tiny bubbles that made him shiver as they cooled. Suddenly unsteady on his feet, he stumbled against her. She shifted her weight, her arm sliding about his waist, and pressed herself against him. Her breasts were surprisingly heavy and firm against his chest. He forgot that she was anything other than a very desirable, apparently willing woman. And it had been an eternity since he'd had a woman in his arms. He tightened the arm around her amazingly narrow waist, not quite certain when he'd placed it there, and felt her lift against him, moaning softly as she went up on tiptoe. Delighted, he slanted his head, grinding his mouth against hers and nuzzling her cheek. Her skin was smooth as silk, her breath hot and sweet. When her tongue licked shyly at the edges of his teeth, he stabbed his own into the damp, dark well of her mouth, shuddering with needs long subdued by the day-to-day difficulties of his life.

She trembled against him, straining ever upward, her fingertips pressing indentations into the skin of his back through the heavy, serviceable fabric of his uniform shirt, her breasts heaving against him as she struggled for breath. He dropped his hand from her nape to her back and slid it beneath her arm to boldly cup one full, firm breast, his own body leaping and swelling painfully at the contact. It was then that she suddenly wrenched away.

He stood there, arms outstretched as if reaching for her, body clamoring, senses reeling. Gradually his head cleared. Mattie stared at him, mouth and eyes wide, as the reality of what he'd done hit him like a blow from a sledgehammer. He had kissed the baby-sitter—the very young, very impressionable Mattie—and she was looking at him now as if he'd hung the moon!

"Oh, Orren!"

Horror swiftly descended. He hadn't just kissed her; he'd touched her breast! "No!" he gasped.

Mattie put her hands together and smiled serenely, as if she'd known all along how devastatingly electric a kiss between them would be. He felt suddenly as if someone had yanked the ground right out from under him.

"No, no, no, no, no!"

She shook her head pityingly and said with terrible patience, "Orren, listen to me."

He literally clapped his hands over his ears. "No way! Oh my God! No way is this going to happen!"

She folded her arms, smirking censoriously. "It already *has* happened."

"No, it hasn't!" he exclaimed. "And it's not going to again!"

She covered her mouth with a hand, and he had the sneaking suspicion that she was hiding a smile, but he had no time to consider the ramifications of that. There were things she had to understand right now, this very instant. He cleared his throat, prepared to be very firm.

"Number one," he said loudly, "I've sworn off women! I don't need that kind of complication in my life. It's already complicated enough, thank you very much. And number two, even if I hadn't and it wasn't, it wouldn't be *you!* You're too young!"

"I'm almost twenty," she argued lightly, dropping her hand.

"You're nineteen! That's a teenager, and that's too young!"

She sighed. "I'm not—"

"Number three!" he interrupted, holding up three fingers to underscore the point. "I don't have time for it!"

"I want to help you have time," she said reasonably, but he thrust his hand in her face before she could say more, four fingers up this time.

"Four, I won't put my kids through it," he said flatly. "I won't get them thinking there's something between us,

I won't get their hopes up like that! It wouldn't work out, and they'd just be disappointed, and I won't do it to them! They've already lost one mother. They won't lose another!"

"No, they won't," she said quietly. "I agree with you there."

He blinked in surprise. "You do?"

She lifted her chin and her eyebrows simultaneously. "Of course, I do. You can't think I'd hurt the children."

He shook his head, a hand stealing up to the back of his neck. "Th-then you agree we can't— We won't—" He took a deep breath. "You understand that it can't happen again?"

She smiled at him, a very Madonnalike smile, all knowing, serene, accepting, and flatly said, "No."

He gaped at her. "No? No?"

She turned on one heel, flipped him a smile over one shoulder and said gaily as she sauntered away, "No."

He stared mutely as she walked to the steps, climbed them, opened the door and went inside. No! *No?* He groaned, imagining a Mattie now intent on making him want her, on provoking a repeat performance, as it were, of what had happened earlier. Somehow it was no longer at all difficult to envision Mattie with a "come-hither" smile playing about her lips, emerald eyes smoldering, mouth parting in anticipation of his kiss. He put his hands to his head. Dear heaven, he'd created a monster!

As if to confirm his fears, the door to the house opened, and Mattie stuck her head out. He dropped his hands, glaring at her. She put on a stern face and hissed, "And speaking of disappointing these kids, the room stays as it is, so just deal with it!" She slammed the door shut again before he could work up any outrage at all, so he didn't even bother to try. Instead, he admitted ruefully that she'd neatly punched holes in his prideful argument about the room with his own insistence that his children be protected from disappointment. Well, all right then. He couldn't have it both ways, so neither could she. The room remained as it was, and he'd chop off his hands before he touched her again. That way, everyone was safe—wasn't he, er, they? He shook his head, pushing away thoughts of how delicious she'd felt in his arms. It simply wouldn't work; he believed it body and soul. Well, mind and soul, anyway. If it took a little longer to convince his body, then so be it, for he would not become romantically involved with Matilda Kincaid. Whatever it took.

"When's Daddy coming home?"

Mattie smiled encouragingly at Jean Marie and brushed a wisp of curly, red hair from her forehead. "I don't know, honey. He said he'd be working late, but he didn't know what time he might be able to get away."

To her relief and delight, Jean Marie leaned into her and looped an arm loosely about her waist, whining, "I wanna ask Daddy if I can go to Ramona's birthday party."

Mattie hugged her, using the need to support Jean Marie's upper body weight as an excuse. "Oh, I think it'll be okay."

"But I got to take a gift," Jean Marie pointed out.

And gifts cost money, Mattie thought. She didn't even consider buying one herself for the child to take to the party, but maybe there was another way. "Tell you what, I have an idea for a really spectacular gift, and it won't cost any money, but you will have to pay for it."

Jean Marie curled up her nose. "If it don't cost money, then how can I pay for it?"

"We'll barter."

"Huh?"

Mattie laughed at the screwed-up face that reflected Jean Marie's confusion. "It works like this, I'll give you two manicures if you'll give me two hours of work."

"What's a mannercure?"

She picked up Jean Marie's small, dry hand and turned it over in her own. "Well, that's where I soak your hands in a special lotion until they're soft as silk. Then I push back your little cuticles..." She demonstrated on two fingers. "And I paint your nails, oh, electric blue, maybe, or lime green, even yellow. Then I make delicate designs on them with glitter and fix them with hardener. And you have the most spectacular hands to show off at that party next week."

Jean Marie's eyes were wide with wonder. "You do it twice for both hands, so they're the same?"

Mattie shook her. "No, one manicure is for you, all ten fingers, and the other is for your friend Ramona. But you have to work to pay for them, two full hours. Agreed?"

Jean Marie was hopping up and down on her feet. "Oh, boy! Oh, boy! It'll be so cool! Ramona will flip! Thank you, Mattie! Thank you!"

Mattie laughed, lifting first one foot and then the other in an effort to spare them torture. "Remember what I said about the work, now. I expect two full hours."

"Yes! Yes! Yes! I promise!"

"Okay, here's what we'll do, then. We'll make a special certificate announcing Ramona's gift, and you can give her that at the party. You can show her your nails, too, so she'll know just what she's getting. And we'll leave a space on the certificate for the date and time when she can get her manicure—I'll work that out with Ramona's mother. Then we'll pick her up and bring her here for her manicure."

"And I can show her my room!" Jean Marie enthused.

"And you can show her your room," Mattie agreed.

Jean Marie leaped up and threw her arms around Mattie's neck, nearly toppling them both. Laughing, Mattie caught her and stumbled back against the kitchen counter, while Jean Marie pecked kisses on her cheek and chin. "Oh, I love you, Mattie. Thank you! Thank you!"

Mattie closed her eyes and squeezed the child tight, whispering, "I love you, too, Red."

When she opened her eyes again, Orren was standing in the doorway, a look of such exhaustion and defeat on his face that the tears burning the backs of her eyes suddenly threatened to flood her cheeks. Sensing his presence, Jean Marie whipped her head around, promptly abandoned Mattie and ran to throw her arms around her father's upper legs, babbling her news. Orren struggled to follow the flow of his daughter's happy words, nodding and murmuring appropriate phrases as he ushered Jean Marie deeper into the house and closed the door.

"And I'm gonna pay for it with two hours of *hard* work," Jean Marie promised, finally winding down.

"That's great, Red," Orren told her. "That's real fine. I bet Ramona will like your gift best of all."

"Then it's okay?" Mattie asked, stepping forward.

His glance bounced off her, decidedly cool. "Sure. Why not?"

She tried not to let it hurt. She knew he was struggling not to let his feelings for her blossom, and she knew, deep down, that he was going to lose that struggle, in which case she could well afford to be generous. "I put back dinner for you."

"Thanks."

Jean Marie scampered off to spread her news, knowing that Chaz could be found in his "room" with a book.

"Yancy and Candy are asleep," Mattie told Orren as she brought his dinner out of the oven. "I promised them you'd kiss them good-night when you came in and make them a special breakfast in the morning."

Orren nodded grimly, saying, "I'll set the alarm a little early," as he moved to the sink to wash up.

"I already have everything ready for you," she informed him, pointing to a small sheet of paper on the counter, "and I've written the instructions down."

He muttered something unintelligible to that. She decided to take it as grateful assent and carefully placed his dinner plate on the table between the folded napkin and the flatware. She pulled forward the small bouquet of wild flowers stuffed into a jelly jar of water decorated with a ribbon woven of grass. "The kids did this for you."

He turned a look over his shoulder and smiled as he dried his hands. "That's sweet."

"They're sweet kids," she said wistfully.

He turned away. "Yes."

Knowing full well that he wouldn't sit down at the table until she moved away from it, Mattie went to the corner of the kitchen and picked up her bag from the counter next to the refrigerator. "Guess I'll be going."

He went to his chair and pulled it out, saying nothing. She hefted the straps of her bag over one shoulder and moved to the door. He sat down and picked up his fork. She opened the door and stepped through it, but she couldn't go without one more word. The kids had told her that he often stayed up late watching television after his long hours of work, and it was telling on him. She backed up and said gently, "Try to get some rest. You need it."

She knew that he heard her, for he went absolutely still, but he said nothing. She sighed, knowing that it was deliberate. Understanding, but determined as well, she said, "Good night, Orren."

She went out and pulled the door closed gently behind her.

Orren sat and stared unseeingly at the food on his plate. Meat loaf. Corn. Mustard greens. Oven-roasted potatoes. Mattie was a good cook. Mattie was a good housekeeper. Mattie was a good baby-sitter. She was driving him nuts, and in many ways he wished he'd never laid eyes on her. But his kids were so happy with her. He'd never seen Red so happy as she was just now. His heart squeezed when he remembered how she'd told Mattie that she loved her. She hardly talked of Gracie anymore. He didn't know if that was good or bad. He only knew that he wasn't going to make the same kinds of mistakes that he'd made in the past. He wasn't going to fall in love with the wrong woman.

Mattie was too young. She couldn't even know yet what she wanted out of life, and he knew that from experience. Gracie had once thought that she wanted to be a wife and a mother, but she had been too young to realize what she was getting into, and she'd been nearly twenty-one at the time, to his nineteen. Orren sighed and made himself eat, even though his appetite had vanished when he'd stepped through the door and found his prickly Red wrapped around Mattie. He didn't want her to win over Red. That was hitting too close to home. If she could win over the hard case, the rest of them were just putty in her hands. But they were young hands, much too young, despite their talent and gentleness. In a flash of memory, he felt those hands on his body again. Ruthlessly, he pushed the remembered sensations away. Too young. She was just too young to be saddled with four kids and a worn-out man whose heart could no longer aspire to the higher emotions. She was too young, and he was too tired, and that was that.

He polished off his dinner and carried the plate to the sink, but he didn't rinse or wash it. He was just too tired, and seeing the kids before they went to sleep was more important. Besides, that's what he paid Mattie for, to cook and clean and watch the kids. He went in Chaz's temporary room and sat on the bed and talked to Chaz and Jean Marie, hearing about their day and the birthday party invitation that had come in the mail for Jean Marie and the book Mattie had loaned Chaz. He promised to watch a movie with them on the VCR in the living room. Then he went in and kissed his baby girls, careful not to wake them. He stood for long minutes and watched them sleep, loving them so much and wishing he could do more than work too much and kiss them in their sleep and make a breakfast somebody else had planned. He wished Gracie had seen in them what he did, instead of just the burden, and he was so tired that tears gathered in his eyes. He sniffed them away and went to shower.

When he came out of the bathroom, dressed in gym

shorts and a T-shirt, the kids had run the movie tape past the previews and warnings and had paused it on the first scene. He snuggled down on the sofa between them and prepared to watch a movie about an Australian cowboy that he'd already seen dozens of times. They were deep into the movie, and he was struggling to stay awake when Chaz suddenly looked up at him and asked, "Dad, why don't you like Mattie anymore?"

Jolted wide awake now, Orren sat up straight and cleared his throat. "What makes you think I don't like Mattie?"

Chaz stared back solemnly. "She says you don't."

Orren tamped down a spurt of irritation. "I don't dislike Mattie," he said carefully. "I just don't..." He swallowed what he'd been about to say. "She's the baby-sitter, Chaz. You guys like her, don't you?"

Chaz nodded. "Yes, we like her."

"We love her," Jean Marie said, folding her arms implacably even as she stared at the television set.

Orren felt dangerously close to shattering and flying into pieces. He struggled for composure. "Well, then, there's no problem, is there?"

They both stared up at him, their frank eyes saying clearly that they didn't understand, but they weren't going to argue. What else could he say to them? That he refused to fall in love again? That their mother had ruined him for other women? He told them exactly what he'd been telling himself. "Mattie's too young."

"Too young for what?" Chaz wanted to know.

Orren felt heat climb into his face and was thankful for the dimmed lights. "T-too young to s-stay on permanently," he said. "In the fall, you'll all be going back to school, Mattie included, and that'll be the end of it."

"Will Mattie come back next summer?" Jean Marie asked softly, her voice revealing naked hope.

Orren swallowed painfully. "I don't know, Red. We'll see." She turned back to stare at the TV, but not quickly enough to keep him from catching the glimmer of tears in her eyes. He dropped an arm around her, pulling her close to his side, and said, "But there's no point in worrying about that now. Fall's still a long way off yet, and you've got to earn that manicure for Ramona's birthday."

Jean Marie smiled and nodded, and this time her interest in the movie was genuine. Orren made himself relax. Fall wasn't really so far away. He could hold on that long. Couldn't he? Yes, for the kids' sakes, he definitely could. He pushed away thoughts of what would come afterward, of the difficulties that lay ahead. No point in borrowing trouble. Who was it, he wondered, who'd said that today has troubles enough of its own? Boy, was he right, whoever he was.

Mattie tapped lightly, then opened the door with her key and let herself in. Orren stood at the stove in his stocking feet. His hair was all mussed. He hadn't shaved. His T-shirt was on inside out. He dropped the spatula, splattering himself with egg, and glared at her. "Mattie!" He lowered his voice to a rough, accusing hiss. "What are you doing here so early?"

He hadn't lightened up in the least. In truth, she had expected no less. It took an awfully hardheaded man to raise four children on his own, and once such a man made his mind up to something, well, it was bound to be difficult to change it, but change it she would, one way or another. She slung her bag onto the table and faced him squarely, hands at her hips. "I have to talk to you."

"No, you don't!"

"About the kids."

That corked his pipe. He turned back to his eggs and began scrambling them furiously. "What about them?"

"I'm worried. About Chaz and Yancy in particular."

He scooted the skillet off the burner and turned to glare at her again. "What's wrong with Chaz and Yancy?"

She walked over to the coffeepot and began making the coffee, saying over one shoulder, "For one thing, Chaz doesn't seem to have any friends his own age. Jean Marie does, and that's good, but Chaz should have, too, and he doesn't, not so far as I can tell, anyway."

For a moment Orren said nothing, but he grumbled, "Of course, he does."

She turned around and leaned back against the counter. "So who are they then? What are their names? Met any of them?"

He looked at her like she'd grown two heads. "I don't know! What difference does it make?"

"It makes a lot of difference," she said firmly, "to Chaz."

She had him worried now. She could tell by the way he paused to stroke his chin. "He's got to have friends. Why wouldn't he? He's a perfectly likable boy."

"Yes, he is," she agreed. "He's also completely wrapped up in his family. He seems to think this family is the sole reason for his existence. I don't think even he realizes that he's missing out on something most little boys have lots of, and that's friends his own age."

Orren's brow furrowed. "Hasn't he mentioned anyone?"

She shook her head. "No. And I've asked."

Orren frowned. "You think this is my fault, I'm sure."

She let that pass as unworthy of comment. "I think we need to expose him to children his own age without his sisters around for him to worry about. And I think Yancy needs the same thing."

He folded his arms. "I happen to know a thing or two about children, Matilda, and I promise you that Yancy isn't old enough yet to worry about friends her own age."

"I agree," she said smoothly. "Yancy isn't old enough to worry about it. But *I'm* old enough to realize that she needs role models her own age even if *you* aren't."

He scowled at that. "What are you talking about?"

She folded her own arms, mimicking his stance, and let him have it. "Yancy needs to grow up, Orren. She's four going on one and a half. If she doesn't gain a little maturity soon, she won't be ready for kindergarten. She needs to be around kids her own age in order to learn what's expected of her. Surely you can see that."

Orren tried another glower, but his concern for his daughter got the better of him. He let his arms slip down to his sides. "Don't you think she'll grow out of it on her own?"

"No, I don't. She's fixated. She just needs a little push in the right direction."

Orren pushed a hand through his already wildly disarranged hair. She could tell he had accepted the truth of her arguments and was castigating himself for not having deduced these problems on his own. He sent her a belligerent glance. "I suppose you can just snap your fingers and come up with the solutions to all our problems," he complained tartly. "You're so good at finding them."

"No more than you," she retorted and immediately regretted it. "Actually, I've had more opportunity and reason than you to think about it," she went on more mildly. "No one can blame you for not seeing such problems when more often than not you're too tired to think when you're here."

He merely frowned and said, "What do you want to do?"

"I want to take them to church," she said, failing to anticipate his explosion.

"To church! What's the matter with you? What's church got to do with it? I don't have time for church! I work six, sometimes seven days a week, for pity's sake!"

"I know that, Orren!" she interrupted his tirade, a bit more shrilly than she'd intended. "I'm not suggesting *you* go to church. Heaven forbid! I'm suggesting you let me take *your children* to church. There is this thing there called Sunday school, where they divide the children according to ages and engage them in age-appropriate activities with a Biblical theme. I'm sure you've heard of it. A man doesn't live to your ripe old age without hearing of it!"

He ground his teeth in an obvious attempt to curb his

temper. "So this is your grand solution?" he finally said. "Sunday school?"

She bit back another angry retort, suddenly ashamed of herself, and took a deep breath. "Yes, I'm afraid it is," she said finally. "You see, I don't know any other eight-year-old boys, and short of enrolling Yancy in day care, I don't know what else to do for her. I thought that Sunday school would give each of them a chance to socialize within their own age groups, and since I go every Sunday, anyway..." She let it tail off, the conclusion obvious.

Orren turned his back on her, his hands going to his hips. After a long while he said, "I suppose I could get them ready if you'll come pick them up."

"All right," she agreed softly.

He nodded, then straightened and walked to the stove to retrieve his cooling eggs. Mattie turned and finished preparing the coffee, then switched on the pot to brew. Orren stuffed bread into the toaster and set it, after scraping his eggs onto a plate. They stood, each in his or her own spot, and listened to the ticking sound of the toaster accompanied by the sucking sound of the coffeepot, until Mattie could bear it no more.

"Orren, I'm sorry!" she blurted out. He jerked as if she'd poked him but kept his face resolutely turned away.

The toast popped up just then, and he snatched it from the toaster, dropped it quickly onto his plate, grabbed up the plate and carried it into the living room. She waited long minutes before she picked up his fork and took it to him.

"You forgot this."

She held the fork out. Without so much as looking up at her, he snatched it out of her hand and stabbed it into the cold egg on the plate balanced atop his knees. Someone cried out, one of the girls, Yancy or Candy Sue from the sound of it. Orren shifted the plate. Mattie dropped a hand onto his shoulder.

"I'll go. Eat your breakfast."

She moved off toward the hallway. At the very last moment he stopped her.

"Mattie."

She didn't turn, merely stood where she was. "Yes?"

"Thank you."

She knew perfectly well what he was thanking her for—and it wasn't the fork. She smiled to herself. A hardheaded man who loved his children above all else. He had room in that heart for a woman; somehow she knew it. And he would know it, too. Somehow.

Chapter Five

"I've told the kids," Orren said, his hand already on the doorknob. "I don't expect I'll be home tonight."

Mattie controlled the first gush of feeling brought on by such news, which was shock, and in so doing succumbed to the rush of the second—concern. "Is something wrong? Can I do anything?"

Irritation flashed over his face. "Nothing's *wrong.* Something's *right.* I've got a special job. A mobile harvester coming through town had a breakdown and needs a diesel engine replaced pronto. The garage doesn't do diesel, but the boss agreed to let me use the shop after hours to get it done on my own. Couple of the boys are going to help me. I expect we'll be at it all night and part of tomorrow night, too."

She knew better than to argue, but she couldn't help it. "Orren, you can't go without sleep that long."

"For a solid two thousand bucks, I can," he declared flatly. "Don't worry, I'll make it worth your while to stay over with the kids."

She could see that it was no use arguing with him. Instead she asked, "Should I bring dinner down to you?"

He shook his head.

"Then how are you going to eat?" The words slipped out before she could stop them.

"Never you mind!" he snapped. "I'm an adult, you know. I can take care of myself. You just take care of the kids."

Mattie wanted to cry. Couldn't he see how much she cared? Of course he could, and that was what infuriated him. She lifted her chin, even as she sighed inwardly, and said, "You know perfectly well that the children will be happy and safe with me—as much as they can be without you."

"That's all I care about," he grumbled, but his gaze no longer challenged hers.

She could feel his gratitude—and his reluctance to admit to it. Shaking her head, she said, "You could be happy and safe with me, too, Orren, if you'd let yourself."

Alarm flared behind his fine blue eyes, followed quickly by denial and an all-too-familiar irritation. "If you were old enough to know what you're talking about—" he began.

Mattie threw up her hands and rolled her eyes, turning away. "Just go!" She stomped over to the sink and wrenched on the tap water, searching among the breakfast dishes for the stopper. "Go on. Make your escape, Orren. I'll be here when you get back. No matter what you do, I'll be here. Because here is where I *want* to be."

He stared at her for a long moment, mouth opening and closing again, as if he would argue or comment or perhaps even apologize, but in the end he just turned and walked through the door. Mattie leaned her forearms on the edge of the countertop and pulled a deep, calming breath, tears burning the backs of her eyes. But she would not cry. She was no child, and she would not let him make her act like one. No matter how hard he tried.

* * *

The television screen flickered silently. Mattie tucked her feet up under her thighs and resisted the urge to glance once more at the clock on the end table before turning the page of the book propped on the arm of the sofa. She already knew that it was well past midnight. Perhaps it was already past one in the morning. She no longer really wanted to know. Every minute now was pure torture. Surely he had caught a few hours sleep at the shop. No one could go this long without rest. Biting her lip, she pushed the worry away, but others crowded in to take its place. What if he fell asleep behind the wheel on his way home? What if he collapsed there alone? What if—

The sudden flare of lights against the kitchen window ricocheted off the end wall of the living area. Mattie leaped up, the book tumbling forgotten to the sofa cushion. Her gaze went automatically to the clock. It was later than she'd thought, ten minutes past two in the morning. But he was home. He was finally home. She sat back down again, relief momentarily washing away her strength, and bowed her head over her hands, quickly thanking God. The sounds of tires rolling over gravel and then an engine idling brought her head up once more. The rumble of the engine died away, and she let out her breath. Calm again, she pulled the book from beneath her and thumbed through the bent pages to find her place, intent on appearing unconcerned when he came inside.

She found her place and stared for long minutes at the printing on the page without deciphering a single word. It was her imagination, of course. Surely only seconds had passed since she'd picked up the book. Chewing her lip, she glanced once more at the clock. Two-twenty! She was on her feet again, the book in her hands this time. Carefully, she bent down the corner of the page and closed the cover. Reverently laying the book aside, she walked sedately to the kitchen door and looked out the small window in it. The headlights of the truck still burned, glaring harshly off the forward wall of the carport. She could just make out Orren's form slumped over the steering wheel. Mattie jerked open the door and ran down the steps to the truck. She opened the cab door easily, without even lifting the latch, and reached inside. Orren shrugged and mumbled at her touch.

"Neetsleemm. Tire."

Relief swept through her for the second time. She clamped a hand onto his forearm and another onto the opposite shoulder, saying, "I know you need sleep. You're worse than tired. You're exhausted. Let's get you to bed."

"Bed," he sighed, letting her pull him out of the truck. His feet hit the carport floor, and he swayed weakly.

Mattie ducked beneath his arm and threw her shoulder against his side. "Come on, big guy. Lean on me. We'll get there."

"Mattie," he said, and shook his head, eyes blinking repeatedly.

"That's right. Good old Mattie. Step up."

He obediently did as told.

"Again."

He took the second step, then stumbled on the threshold. They staggered together into the house. "I got it. I got it," he muttered. Leaning against the wall, he exhaled deeply and ran a hand over his face. "Where're my kids?"

Mattie slid an arm around his waist and pushed him away from the wall. "Sleeping, of course, tucked all safe in their beds, which is where you need to be."

He yawned, lifting a fist to cover it but not quite getting there. "We did it," he said and fumbled in his pants pocket, swaying and extracting a wad of bills as big as a baseball. He shoved it at her, pushing it up under her chin. "Twenty-three," he told her sluggishly. "Hundred."

Mattie attempted to push it away, only to find herself holding it.

"God, I'm tired," he said, laying his head back against the wall. "Can't b'lieve I made it home."

"You shouldn't have tried it in this shape," Mattie scolded lightly, reaching across him to stuff the bills back into his pocket.

He caught her hand and pressed it against his body, swaying forward so that his nose bumped her temple, his hot breath gusting into her ear. "What're you doing to me?" he whispered.

Mattie jerked her hand free, her heart suddenly pounding, and gritted out, "Trying to get you into bed."

His arms came around her loosely, his weight sagging against her. "I'm too tired to fight you, Mattie," he said in a lazy drawl. "And I don't really want to."

She tightened her arm around his waist and tried to ignore the heat pooling in her lower body. "Then don't," she said matter-of-factly, and tugged him away from the wall once more. They staggered around the kitchen table and into the living room. She glanced up and noted that he was staring longingly at the sofa. "Oh, no," she said. "We're putting you to bed. We've gotten this far. We can manage the rest of the way. Come on."

He growled low in his throat, but he straightened and took some of his weight off her. Together they slowly walked across the living room, his steps dragging, and into the hallway. She let him pause in the doorway to his bedroom. Sighing, he leaned a shoulder against the frame and pushed a hand through his hair. "Will I hear the kids?" he asked, confused.

She pulled him away from the door frame, afraid to let him get too comfortable just yet. "The kids will be fine," she promised, leading him toward the bed. "I'll be here when they get up."

"You're always here," he muttered. "Sweet Mattie. Too good. What'll we do withou' you?"

"I'm not going anywhere," she said, pushing him onto the bed with her hip. She intended to let him down easily, leveraging his weight against her shoulders with both hands clamped onto his wrist, but he sagged and then collapsed unexpectedly, pulling her down with him and trapping the arm about his waist beneath him on the bed. She landed against him with an "Oof."

He groaned and attempted to roll over onto his side, carrying her along with him, his arm curled around her shoulders. "Mattie," he said, just that, but imbued with a satisfaction that gladdened her heart. She slipped a hand into the curve of his neck and laid her head against his chin, holding him while his breathing steadied and slowed. But she dared not stay there too long. Already her trapped arm was cramping. Reluctantly, she struggled up into a sitting position and pulled herself free. He muttered something and threw an arm across his face.

Mattie scooted off the bed and quickly stripped his shoes and socks from his feet. Next she unbuttoned his shirt and pulled him up by it, pushing it back off his shoulders. He awakened enough to shrug out of it and fumbled with his pants, getting them open and down over his hips. Mattie quickly averted her gaze, then reached down and grasped his pants by the hems, tugging them down his legs. He found the pillow and crawled onto it, folding his arm beneath it. She yanked and tugged and pulled the covers down beneath him, then carefully pulled them upward again, to his shoulders, her gaze preceding them. Heavens, he was beautiful, all solidly packed muscle in smoothly sculpted contours. No wonder he was so heavy! She brushed several locks of hair off his forehead, studying his face. It was a strong face, as hard and firm as the rest of him, and yet somehow vulnerable. She ached for the exhaustion that had claimed him, for the desperation that had driven him to it. Love swelled her heart almost painfully.

It had been building inside her for some time, perhaps from the first moment she'd met him, and with it came the certainty that she belonged with him. Had her mother felt this for her father? she wondered. Somehow Mattie knew that she had. Amy must have felt it, too. The thought made Mattie glad. She wanted Amy to feel this way for her father. She wanted him to be loved like this. He was as good a man as Orren, as deserving, as responsible and loving, as dedicated a father—and as stubborn. Smiling at the thought, she shook her head. No wonder Orren felt so right for her. She was used to dealing with just his sort of pigheaded determination. She appreciated it as only the daughter of an equally pigheaded father could. Smiling still, she bent closer and lightly pressed her lips to Orren's.

He shifted onto his back, and before she knew what was happening, his arms came up and enfolded her, pulling her down to him. He settled onto his side, putting her back to the bed, and for a moment he drew away. His eyes opened and stared into her surprised face. "Mattie," he said, "I knew you'd be here." And then his mouth sought hers again in a kiss fraught with sweetness and hunger and a depth of longing she had only guessed at.

She told herself that she ought not to take such advantage of him. His defenses were weakened by exhaustion. Weeks of proximity had worn him down. Nevertheless, she wound her arms around his neck and gave back as good as she got, telling him without words that she loved and wanted him. After a long, lazy while, his mouth slid from hers and he drew breath, sighing as he nuzzled her cheek. His hand wandered up her side and cupped her breast.

"You're not a child," he said softly into her ear.

Smiling and blinking at tears, she pressed her face into the curve of his neck. In only moments, he slipped again into deep sleep. She lay next to him, very much at peace, until her eyes began to grow heavy and she knew she had to go or spend the night here. Reluctantly, she extricated herself and scooted to the foot of the bed. Orren flung an arm out as if looking for her, muttered in his sleep, and settled down again. Mattie pulled the window shade to block the morning light and tiptoed from the darkened room, gently closing the door behind her. As she moved through the house, shutting off the television and turning out the few remaining lights, she tried not to wonder what would happen with them now.

Would he remember tomorrow what he had said and done tonight? Would he admit what he felt for her? Was it what she hoped it was?

She pushed away the questions and concentrated on getting safely home. After parking in the driveway, she let herself into the house and crept down the hall to her room. Just as she reached it, the door to her father's room opened, and Evans stepped into the hallway, belting his robe.

"You're awfully late, Mattie. Is everything okay?"

"Everything's fine, Dad," she told him fondly. "Go back to bed."

"I expected you earlier," he said, yawning.

She reached around the end of the wall and flipped on the light in her room, saying, "Orren worked forty-one straight hours. He barely made it home."

Evans blinked at the light. "That boy works too hard, and he's imposing on you."

"He isn't imposing, Dad," she said. "I love being out there with the kids. Now go back to sleep. I have to be up early to get the kids ready for Sunday school."

"You're taking them to church?"

"Yes."

"*He* going, too?"

She shook her head, smiling at the emphasis her father could inject into a simple personal pronoun. "Orren needs to sleep. Maybe next week."

Evans grunted at that. "Mattie, you're getting too involved with these people."

Sighing, she went up on tiptoe and kissed him on the chin. "You don't really want to talk about this now, do you?"

He grumbled that she shouldn't stay out so late, said good-night and slipped back into the room that he shared with Amy. Mattie went into her room and closed the door, stripped off her clothes, set her alarm, turned off the light, and slid between the sheets. Her last thought as she drifted into sleep was that she felt oddly out of place in her own bed, and she wondered if either Evans or Orren could understand why.

The alarm went off entirely too early. Mattie groaned and rolled over to swat it into silence. Yawning and stretching, she got out of bed and wandered into the shower. She was gone before her father or Amy so much as stirred.

She let herself into Orren's house, tied a towel around her waist and began preparing breakfast. When it was ready, she went to check on Orren before waking the children. He was dead to the world, his chin and jaws covered with a rough growth of dark beard. She kissed him lightly, got no response and slipped away to rouse the children, shushing them as she eased them from slumber with kisses and whispers, Chaz first, then Jean Marie and the babies. While they ate breakfast, she laid out their clothes and lined up their toothbrushes, squeezing the paste onto them to save time. She ushered Chaz into the bathroom first, then quickly pried him out again, sending in Jean Marie, who proved a little more difficult to dislodge. Yancy and Candy Sue required more supervision, but she managed to have them washed and brushed and dressed in time to help Chaz tuck in his shirttail and weave Jean Marie's hair into a French braid that lay neatly against her head. Through it all she repeatedly explained that Orren had worked two full days and almost two full nights to bring in extra money for them and that he deserved to sleep undisturbed.

"Besides," she told Chaz, "you'll like Sunday school. There are some nice boys in your class."

Unconvinced, he nevertheless helped her get everyone into their shoes and headed for the car. She dashed off a note to Orren in case he woke while they were gone, propped it in the center of the kitchen table and whisked out of the house with just enough time to make it to church.

Chaz proved surprisingly shy, but Mattie left him in the

capable hands of her pastor's wife. Clarice Charles was a lovely, charming woman, very polished but very warm and the mother of two children, one of them a son. She had easily integrated Chaz into the group, gathering around the piano, by the time Mattie introduced an obviously eager Jean Marie to the class next door. Yancy took a little more cajoling. Putting her thumb into her mouth, she turned her face into Mattie's belly and wrapped her arms around Mattie's leg, shaking her head when asked if she would like to play with the other children.

Mattie went inside and sat down with Candy Sue on one knee and Yancy on the other. Gradually, Yancy responded to the overtures of the teachers and other children. When Mattie slipped away, Yancy was sitting on the floor in a semicircle with her contemporaries, listening intently to the story that the teacher was telling with the aid of paper dolls lightly fixed to a felt background.

Candy Sue, unfortunately, was now wise to the process, and while she showed no great reluctance to meet the teachers or children in her own class next to the nursery, she also displayed no intention of letting go of Mattie. Indeed, she seemed to have grown extra arms and legs, attaching a new one as Mattie gently pried loose another. She giggled at the teacher, who called her an angel, and grabbed hold of Mattie's hair with both hands. The pastor, Bolton Charles, stuck his head in the door just then, raising both eyebrows when he spied Mattie there.

"What's this, a new fashion accessory?" he teased, playfully poking Candy Sue in the ribs. She giggled and correspondingly tightened her hold on Mattie. "My goodness, she is a little beauty, isn't she?"

"Oh, yes, she is, and she knows it, too," Mattie told him. "This is the Reverend Charles, honey. Can you say hello?"

Candy nodded and said, "Hello."

Bolton Charles laughed. "Hello, young lady. What's your name?"

"Sweetums."

"Sweetums!" Bolton teased. "Who gave you a name like that? Someone sweet on you, I'll bet."

"My daddy."

"Well, no wonder," Bolton said. "It fits!"

Mattie shook her head, smiling, and said, "Actually, it's Candy Sue Ellis. Sweetums is a nickname."

"Ellis," Bolton mused, stroking his chin. "I don't believe I know any Ellis family."

Mattie shrugged. "I just met them this summer myself."

Bolton nodded. "Well, I'm glad to see that you've brought Miss Candy Sue to church. Can we expect Mom and Dad anytime soon?"

"Dad, maybe." She grinned coyly. "I'm working on him."

Bolton cocked his head and said softly, "I take it Mom's not around any longer."

Candy Sue spoke up, exclaiming, "Mommy's gone, gone." She extended her little arm and flipped her hand as if to say that Mommy had disappeared into thin air.

Mattie leaned close to the handsome minister and said quietly, "She went off with another man more than two years ago."

Bolton shook his head sadly. "I'm sorry to hear that."

"There are four children, Reverend Charles," she went on softly. "Candy's the youngest at three. They're the sweetest things. I just don't understand."

"Maybe we can't understand, Mattie," he told her gently, "but we shouldn't judge, either."

"I know, but I see how hard their father works to take care of them, and I can't help wondering how she could do it. It's obvious he was crushed when she left."

The Reverend Charles was a wise man. He looked straight into Mattie's exotic eyes and asked, "How old would you say he is?"

She answered nonchalantly, "Twenty-eight."

The minister was surprised. "That's young."

She nodded. "But not too young. He's totally dedicated. He loves his family."

Candy Sue apparently decided that it was time the conversation centered on her again. She seized Mattie's face between her two little hands and tugged her head down for a noisy kiss, declaring, "I wuv you, Mattie!"

Mattie laughed and put her forehead to Candy's. "You aren't going to let go, are you, Sweetums?"

Candy laughed and shook her head. "I wanna be wif you."

Mattie shrugged at Bolton. "Guess I could take her into my class this once." She switched her gaze to Candy again, adding, "But only if you promise to be very, very good."

Candy nodded solemnly and laid her head on Mattie's shoulder. Bolton let them out into the hallway and followed them down the hall. Mattie could feel the care with which he chose his words. "Seems you've made at least one conquest."

She smiled and turned a look over her shoulder, admitting honestly, "I'm aiming for five."

They had reached the bottom of the stairs that led up to the second floor of what was designated as the education building. Mattie set Candy on her feet. The child was just too heavy to carry up a full flight of stairs. Besides, maybe the climb would tire her out so that she'd sit quietly once they arrived at the classroom. Meanwhile, Bolton Charles was studying Mattie with frank curiosity. Finally he said, "Mr. Ellis must be quite a gentleman."

Mattie smiled. "Yes. Very special. In fact, he's just like my father."

Bolton chuckled. "That's high praise, indeed!"

"I don't think Dad would agree," she told him wryly.

Bolton nodded thoughtfully. "Should I be praying about this?"

"Couldn't hurt."

"Never does," he told her, a comforting hand patting her shoulder.

"Say an extra one for Orren," she requested softly.

"That's Mr. Ellis?"

"Yes. He worked forty-one straight hours starting Friday morning, and that was after putting in a full week."

The reverend raised his dark brows. "You said he was dedicated."

"That's not all. He's also stubborn, hardheaded, honorable to a fault, proud, independent.... Like I said—"

"Just like your father."

"Exactly."

"Sounds like you have your eyes wide open, Mattie."

"I think so."

The reverend put his hands behind his back and leaned forward, muttering conspiratorially, "Does he know how lucky he is?"

She laughed and flipped her hair off her shoulder, Candy's little hand in hers. "I'm working on it."

Bolton smiled. "I'll say an extra prayer for you, too."

"Thanks."

Someone down at the end of the hall hailed him then, and he backed away, flipping a wave to Mattie and another to Candy. Candy Sue waved back and turned up the stairs at Mattie's side.

She was good as gold through Bible study, sitting quietly in Mattie's lap. It helped that everyone made a fuss over her lavishly before they began. Mattie checked before worship to make certain that the other children had settled happily into children's Church. Yancy was holding hands with the little girl next to her. Jean Marie was whispering into the ear of her seat mate, and Chaz was giggling with his. Pleased, Mattie attempted to coax Candy Sue into joining her own age group for the service, but Candy begged to stay with her, and Mattie easily caved in, reasoning that the little girl had been quiet and polite throughout the first hour. Surely she would remain so through the second. "Next time, though," Mattie stated firmly, "you have to promise that you'll go in with the other girls and boys."

Candy put a hand over her little heart and vowed, "I pwomise."

Mattie knew she was being manipulated shamelessly, but she really didn't mind. She slipped into the back pew with the child, spying her father and Amy near the front. Candy did become a little restless after the music ended and Bolton began to preach, but she was easily entertained with a pencil and an outline of her own hand. Mattie drew a face on one finger of the outline and gave it riotously curly hair, then handed the pencil to Candy, who scribbled industriously until she'd decorated all the other fingers and drawn an odd shape alongside them. "That's Daddy," she whispered, pointing to the tallest finger, "an' Chaz an' Jean M'rie an' Yancy." She pointed the pencil at the extra figure and whispered, "Tha's you!" Obviously, she'd decided that the curly-headed one was herself. Mattie hugged her close and shushed her with a finger pressed to her lips. Candy Sue copied the gesture, drew her feet up into Mattie's lap, and went to sleep with the pencil and paper clutched in her hands.

She seemed to weigh more than her father by the time the service ended and Mattie was able to rise and carry her from the chapel. Luckily, Candy Sue roused when they went to collect the other children, and the four entertained each other for some time, proudly showing off papers and discussing new friends and experiences as Mattie ushered them through the building and out onto the sidewalk. Evans Kincaid swooped down upon her instantly, Amy trailing in his wake.

"Mattie! We didn't see you anywhere in church."

"We were in the back," Mattie said casually. "Candy decided she was going to be a leech today, so I kept her with me."

"Brick was looking for you," Evans said, sounding aggrieved.

"Well, he didn't find me. Oh, let me introduce you. Children you remember my stepmother, don't you?"

"Yes."

"Hello, Mrs. Kincaid. Oh, you should see my room!" This from Jean Marie.

"I'm sure it's lovely."

"I have a yellow wall," Yancy said importantly.

"Pink," was all Candy Sue felt inclined to say.

Mattie lined them up. "Children, this is my father, Officer Evans Kincaid. He's a policeman. Dad, this is Chaz."

"Hello."

They shook hands, Evans obviously ill at ease, Chaz a little shy.

"So should we call you *Officer* Kincaid?" Jean Marie asked, screwing up her face.

"That's right," Mattie told her, a hand on her shoulder. "This is Jean Marie."

"We call her Red," Chaz divulged with a touch of mischief.

Jean Marie took offense, sticking out her tongue. "That wasn't necessary," Mattie said, mildly scolding both, so that Chaz mumbled an apology and Jean Marie bowed her head, shuffling her feet in place. Mattie moved on to the next introduction, first gently pulling the little girl's thumb from her mouth. "This is Yancy. She's four. And Candy Sue is three."

"That's putting them pretty close together, isn't it?" Evans muttered. Mattie politely ignored him.

"They've been perfect little ladies and gentlemen this morning. I think we'll have to have a special dessert for dinner."

Suddenly animated, the children clapped their hands. Evans frowned. "You aren't going to spend the day out there again, are you?"

Mattie glanced up. "Yes, Dad, I am. Orren needs the rest. Someone has to watch the children."

She could tell that he wanted to argue, but the place was too public. She ushered the children along the walkway until they came to stand in front of the pastor. She made the introductions all over again, smiling at Bolton Charles as he complimented the girls and shook Chaz's hand. "I'm looking forward to meeting your father," he told Chaz. "Mattie says he's quite a fellow."

Chaz puffed out his chest proudly. "He rebuilt a whole diesel engine! He fixes stuff all the time!"

"Sounds handy," Bolton said, smiling at Mattie.

"He's building on to the house," Chaz went on. "I got my own room!"

"It's not finished yet," Mattie explained, "but it shouldn't be long now."

"He worked real hard and made a bunch of money!" Jean Marie said, not to be outdone.

The younger girls just stared up at him, one attached to each of Mattie's legs. Bolton Charles chuckled and said, "Takes a strong young man to manage all that and four children, too."

"Yeah, well, he's had Mattie for that," Evans said none too kindly.

"He couldn't have found better help," Bolton said heartily. "You handle them like they're your very own, Mattie. You could well be their mother."

The entire group went dead silent. Mattie could feel Evans's shock and dismay, as well as the children's innocent speculation. Amy stepped into the breach, saying brightly, "We'd better move on. We don't want to monopolize the reverend. Bolton, you and Clarice must come over for dinner. Evans loves to fire up the grill."

"We'd like that," Bolton told her, squeezing her hand gratefully. "Mattie, I'll remember those prayers you requested."

"Thank you, Reverend."

Quickly, she herded the children toward the parking lot, but her father caught her before they made the sidewalk, one hand falling heavily on her shoulder. "Oh, look," he said much too pointedly, "there's Brick now."

Mattie groaned softly. "Don't, Dad, please."

He gave her a look of patent confusion. "Brick's a friend," he said lightly.

"I don't have time for this now, Dad. I'll see Brick later."

He let her go, but she could hear him arguing in harsh whispers with Amy. She piled the kids into the car, buckled them up, and got behind the wheel. She fit the key into the ignition and switched on the engine.

"Mattie," Chaz said softly from the seat next to her, "you really could be our mother."

She reached out and squeezed his hand, whispering, "I'd like that."

"Me, too," he said huskily.

Blinking back tears, she put the transmission in Reverse and eased the car out into traffic. Her father was standing on the curb when she drove by. He didn't wave, and he didn't smile. Mattie sighed and pointed the car toward home, the Ellis home.

She parked in the drive behind Orren's truck and got everybody out. Candy latched on to her neck and wouldn't let go, so Mattie wagged her into the house on her hip, Yancy clinging to her dress tail, Chaz clutching one hand, while Jean Marie lightly clasped the other. It seemed she'd been adopted—or grafted, she couldn't tell which. It was Jean Marie who asked, as Mattie helped her undress, "Would you really like to be our mother?"

Mattie sat down on the edge of her bed and nodded. "Yes, I would. Know what else? I wouldn't mind being mommy to one or two other children, either."

Jean Marie's eyes went wide. "That many?"

"Why not? I like children. But, Jean, none of this talk means anything. I want you and your brother and sisters to understand that. It was just an idle comment, nothing more."

Jean Marie looked her straight in the eye. "You mean Daddy doesn't love you?"

Mattie had to look away. "I don't know," she said honestly and got up before an even more disturbing question could be asked. "I have to start dinner."

She went out of the room and down the hall toward the living room, but at the last moment, she opened the door to Orren's room. He jerked and rolled over, struggling up on one elbow. Mattie quickly slipped inside and closed the door.

"Go back to sleep," she whispered. "I'll wake you when dinner's ready."

"Mattie," he said. Wiping both eyes, he eased back down and looked her over. "You look good. Never seen you in a real dress before."

She looked down at the simple tea-length cotton print dress, blushing. And to think of all the revealing outfits she'd put together for his benefit! "Thanks. It's just a Sunday dress, nothing special."

He ignored that, saying, "You put me to bed last night."

Her heart sped up just a little bit. She hugged the wall with the palms of both hands. "Do you remember much about it?"

"Enough," he said, holding her gaze for long moments.

She could hardly breathe. She had to swallow before she could speak. "Rest a little longer. I'm going to change and start dinner. I'll wake you when it's ready."

"Kids okay?"

"They're fine," she said. "I think they enjoyed church. They behaved beautifully."

He smiled. "Good." He eased over onto his side and tucked both hands beneath his cheek. He didn't look at all innocent in that pose. Mattie gulped again and went out the door.

Oddly, she wondered if Bolton Charles could be praying for her that very moment. She pictured him at the dinner table with his family, their hands joined, heads bowed. "From your lips to God's ear," she whispered, but in the back of her mind she was hearing Jean Marie ask again, "Doesn't Daddy love you?"

She closed her eyes. "Oh, please," she whispered. "Please. Please."

Chapter Six

"Or-r-ren."

The sound of his own name flowed over him with the silky caress of an ocean breeze. He looked down into Mattie's pixyish face, feeling again the impact of her exotically tilted eyes, so green they seemed unreal. Hair like dark satin framed her head and waved in glossy rumples about her neck and shoulders. Her gently pointed chin was lifted in determination, her wide, pink lips curved in a serene smile.

"Or-r-ren."

He wondered, as he lowered his head to kiss her, how she could speak his name without moving her lips, then lost the thought in the feel of her body against his. She felt wonderful beneath him, her long slender legs tangled with his, her lower body cradling him, her firm breasts pillowing his chest, her arms holding him securely. She seemed both unbelievably delicate and comfortingly substantial. He was aware of her as never before, as a woman, very much a woman.

"Or-r-ren. Orren."

Her voice held a quiet, awesome love, the kind for which he had longed but never believed he could find. She was the mother his mother ought to have been, the sister who had never existed, his best friend, his wife. She was himself, complete. He deepened the kiss, luxuriated in it, but a nagging thought persisted. How could she call his name while kissing him?

"Orren. Wake up. Orren. Orren."

He opened his eyes and looked up into Mattie's pixyish face. Her sleek, dark hair flowed around her face and over her shoulders smoothly. Her exotic green eyes sparkled at him. Her chin tilted inquiringly. Her rose pink mouth curved into a loving smile. He remembered the taste of her, vividly, and forgot all the reasons he should not taste her again. It was a simple matter to arrange it. He merely sat up, took her in his arms and put his mouth to hers. Her smile parted for him, fitting itself to his lips, allowing the teasing forays of his tongue as he sought to taste her mouth. Her hands smooth and lightly calloused, surprisingly strong clutched at his bare back. He folded her closer, seeking and finding the firm mounds of her breasts against his chest. The world shifted a little, skewing and yet somehow righting itself. Her hands slipped around to his shoulders, pressing him back as she pulled away.

She laughed softly. "Dinner's ready. The kids are hungry. Time to get up."

He balanced himself on his elbows. Dinner? Get up? "What time is it?"

"After one."

He absorbed the natural daylight flooding his room. One o'clock in the afternoon! He threw off the bed covers and jackknifed to his feet. Mattie took one look, popped up off the side of his bed and whirled around. Suddenly he recalled every slow, heavy detail of how she'd put him to bed the night before. He felt her hands push his shirt from his shoulders, felt his pants skimming down his legs, the pillow beneath his head, the covers sliding up over his bare skin. In the very same instant, he realized he was standing there in nothing but his briefs. He grabbed the bedcovers and yanked them in front of him, croaking, "Gimme a minute."

Nodding, she escaped the room. Orren stood there with his heart pounding. For a long moment, confusion clouded his mind, but then a certain thought formed. Mattie Kincaid was young, but she was no child. The world had indeed shifted, and he couldn't fight the mental adjustment to the new perspective. The current shape of his body clearly demonstrated that it was well ahead of whatever passed for his mind in this matter. His man's body knew a real woman when it sensed her. What, he wondered, was he going to do with her now that he could no longer pretend she didn't exist?

What he did, eventually, was pull on jeans, socks, a T-shirt and athletic shoes, then make a quick trip to the bathroom for some basic preparation before joining his family at the dinner table. Mattie had found a tablecloth somewhere. He vaguely remembered seeing it before. The table was laid with precise elegance, even though no single place setting matched another, and his children sat in their places with smiling faces and hands folded over the napkins in their laps. That in itself was enough to make him wonder if he'd wandered into the wrong house. The faces that turned up for his kisses were pleasant and not in the least demanding. Even his Sweetums failed to latch on to him like the proverbial leech she invariably became after his prolonged absence. Instead, she giggled in greeting and smacked him on the cheek, giggling some more.

Yancy was talking. "We wents to Sunny school, an' they was bunches of kids an' songs an' stories an' paper dolls an' a girl name Eva an' the tall man said Mattie is our mommy."

"Was like our mommy," Red put in.

"Could be our mommy," Chaz clarified at the same time.

Orren looked up in shock to find Mattie's cheeks turning a beguiling shade of pink, but she held his gaze steadily for a moment before switching it to the baby.

"Candy, why don't you tell Daddy what you did in Sunday school?"

Candy Sue pointed a damp finger at Mattie and said, "I sits in you lap."

"And why did you do that?"

Candy Sue gave her an odd look. "I luv you."

Mattie smiled. "No, sweetheart, I mean, why didn't you stay and play with the children your own age?"

"'Cause I luv you."

Mattie leaned across the table and cupped a hand under Candy's pudgy chin, eliciting another giggle. "I love you, too." She straightened and looked at Orren, shrugging. "I took her to class and worship service with me because she wouldn't let go of me when I tried to leave her in her classroom."

He looked at Candy Sue with a lifted eyebrow. "Sometimes she grows little suckers and attaches herself but good. I think she took lessons from an octopus."

"Well, she promised me that next time she'll go in and play with the other children. Isn't that right, Candy Sue?"

Candy Sue nodded vigorously. Chaz and Jean Marie groaned. "She won't do it," Jean Marie said.

"Yes, she will," Mattie said, leaving no doubt that she'd enforce that promise whether Candy Sue meant to keep it or not. Candy Sue's head came up a little higher, and she traded a look with Jean Marie that said, "Whoops! Got myself in it now." Seeing the exchange, Yancy laughed. Candy Sue put her chin down in the center of her plate. Orren decided that it was time to change the subject. It wasn't hard to find another topic with his stomach pitching a fit for food.

"Dinner looks good. What is that?"

"Chicken and dumplings."

"Oh, yeah." He pulled out his chair and sat down, then

could have kicked himself. He bounced right back up again and stepped around to pull out Mattie's chair for her. He'd have done better to let it go. The kids all looked at one another with silent comment, and Mattie suddenly looked at him with misty eyes. He felt heat climbing his throat. By the time Mattie took her seat and he'd helped her scoot the chair up under the table sufficiently, the heat was pulsing in his face. He hurried around to his own chair and dropped into it, bowing his head without preliminary and rushing into the blessing.

"Lord, thank you for this food and for letting me earn that extra money." He opened his mouth to add an *Amen* and heard himself saying, "A-and thank you for my kids." He figured after that he might as well go whole hog. "And thank you for our home, too. I didn't have a proper home or a real family when I was a boy, so You know they mean the world to me now." Once more, he thought he was finished, but then he felt compelled to add just one more line. It took considerably more breath than the others, so he paused to fill his lungs before saying, "And thank you for Mattie for what she's meant to all of us and because she made this meal for us with her own hands." That felt right, finally, so he closed with, "Amen."

Chaz echoed his *Amen* with one of his own. Orren figured it was something he'd heard done at church that morning, but for some reason it kind of choked him up. He cleared his throat and opened his napkin over his lap. When he looked up, it was to find the kids staring at Mattie. Her head was still bowed. She appeared to be wiping a tear from her eye with the tip of her little finger. He wasn't sure why he did it, but he slid his foot forward until it touched hers beneath the table. She turned and lifted her head. He knew right then, looking into her clear green eyes, that more had changed than he'd realized. Somehow Mattie Kincaid had worked her way into his heart.

To his surprise, the moment passed smoothly. Mattie turned her head and lifted the spoon out of a bowl of sweet corn, reaching for Candy Sue's plate. Orren followed her lead, reaching for Jean Marie's plate and spooning chicken and white doughy dumplings in rich cream gravy onto it. Working together they got the kids' plates filled and attended to their own in only minutes. For a time everyone concentrated on eating, then Chaz put down his fork, wiped his mouth and said, "Dad, would it be all right if I went over to Paul Dotson's house tomorrow? He doesn't live far, and his mom said it would be okay."

Orren resisted the urge to look at Mattie. "Is Paul someone you met at church this morning, son?"

"Well, I knew him before from school, but this morning was when he asked me over."

"I see." He made himself eat another bite before speaking to Mattie. "You know these folks, Mattie?"

"Yes. They've been longtime members of the church. I've sat with the kids. They live about two miles west."

"You reckon it'd be okay for Chaz to go over to play for a while?"

"I'm sure it would be just fine. In fact, I'll call tomorrow and arrange a time, if you like."

He could sense her satisfaction. Well, she was due it. "That'll be just fine. Thanks. So, Chaz, if it all works out, you can go."

Chaz beamed, his excitement palpable, so much so that Jean Marie caught a strong whiff of it. "I want to go, too!" she exclaimed. "Why can't I go, too?"

Orren shook his head lightly. "This is Chaz's friend, Red. He didn't demand to go along with you to the birthday party."

"Actually," Mattie said, "we girls could plan a trip to the park while Chaz is at Paul's if that suits everyone."

Yancy sat up straight and clapped her hands. Candy Sue's beetled brow clearly indicated that she wished she'd been paying better attention. Red bit her lip. Orren could see that she was fighting a battle with herself. He decided to help her along. "That sounds real fine to me. Wish I could go. How 'bout you, Sweetums? You want to go to the park to play tomorrow? They've got those great swings and a big merry-go-round."

Candy Sue finally got it. She dropped her fork in her eagerness to add her clapping to Yancy's. Jean Marie caved in. "Okay," she said, making it clear that she knew she was being manipulated but had decided to be magnanimous anyway.

Orren winked at Chaz, who grinned ear to ear. Orren smiled and went back to his meal, but his mind wasn't on the melt-in-his-mouth chicken. He couldn't help thinking that Matilda Kincaid was awfully good for the Ellis family...all of them. He'd obviously been wrong: she wasn't too young at all.

Mattie began gathering the dishes and carrying them to the sink. Orren and the kids got up to help her, making short work of it, but when she began running hot water into the sink, Orren casually walked over and shut off the spigot.

"Hold on now, everyone," he said to the room at large. "We need a family conference."

The children paused in various stages of the cleanup. Candy Sue was trying to push her chair up under the table and out of the way. Yancy stood holding a clump of wadded paper napkins over the trash can, while Jean Marie closed the cabinet door after returning the salt and pepper shakers to their designated places. Chaz was washing down the table with a wet paper towel. He looked over his shoulder at his father, paused and turned his back to the table. "Want we should sit down at the table again, Dad?"

"That'll work," Orren said. Chaz quickly finished scrubbing the table and put the paper towel in the trash. Yancy dropped her clump and went back to her place. Candy Sue climbed back up into her chair. Only Jean Marie stood where she was, her narrowed gaze on Mattie.

"I'll just finish these," Mattie began, reaching for the

dish soap, but Orren stopped her once more, his hand clamped firmly around her wrist.

"I'll help you later," he said. "Right now I want your opinion on something."

Mattie glanced at Jean Marie. For once, she couldn't tell what the girl was thinking. Her face was carefully blank as she walked to her place, pulled out her chair and dropped down on its edge. Something was brewing there, but Mattie had no idea what. Neither did she suspect what Orren was up to.

Once everyone had resumed their places, Orren cleared his throat, reached into his pocket and tossed a fat wad of bills into the center of the table. A hushed chorus of *wows!* went up. Mattie tilted her head at Orren inquiringly. He folded his hands and nodded at the roll of bills.

"So what're we going to do with it?" he asked.

Chaz and Jean Marie looked at each other. Chaz opened his mouth, but Jean Marie beat him to it. "Put it up for Christmas!"

"Finish my room!"

"You mean my room, don't you, son?" Orren said with a smile. "That's a given." He peeled off several bills and set them aside. "Now then, Christmas is a good idea, Red, but I've already got a savings account for that. They deduct a little bit out of my pay each week especially for Santa Claus." Yancy and Candy Sue exchanged excited glances over that, then turned their gazes back to the money in the center of the table. "What I've been thinking," Orren said, "is that we ought to put this to work for us. The question is how?"

"You could go rodeoing again, Daddy," Chaz said without much enthusiasm.

Orren chuckled at that. "Son, my rodeoing days ended a long time ago. I don't want to go off and leave my family. Besides, I've got a good job."

"You could open your own garage on the side," Jean Marie volunteered.

"No need, Red. I already get work on the side, and my boss lets me use the shop when I need to. No, what I've been thinking is that I ought to buy a few head of cattle."

"You mean we're not going to sell the land?" Chaz asked, an undercurrent of excitement in his voice.

"I've been wondering about that For Sale sign," Mattie said, looking to Orren.

Orren shrugged. "After I had to sell off the cattle last time," he said, "I figured there wasn't any need to just sit on the land. But no one seems to want to buy."

"Did you list it with a Realtor?"

"For a time," Orren said. "He did bring me a couple of offers, but they were on the low side, and I figured we could sit tight for a spell longer."

"You didn't really want to let it go, did you?" Mattie asked, smiling.

Orren tilted his head. "Guess not. Before Gracie— Before my divorce, we were doing pretty good, and I had this idea that we could breed some stock, sell it off to buy more land and eventually have a profitable little ranch going on the side. But the house was really too small, especially when our little Sweetums came along, so I diverted the profits, such as they were at that point, into building. Then the divorce came and things got tight, what with the cost of the divorce and some other things, not to mention child care and all that."

"And you sold off what cattle you'd been able to acquire."

"And put the land up for sale," he confirmed. "But then you came along and this rush diesel job fell in my lap."

"Me!" Mattie said, surprised. "I should think I've been a liability."

Orren let his mouth part in an obvious show of surprise. "Are you kidding? Not only are you cheaper than day care, you've cut the grocery bill by two-thirds, and we're eating better than we ever have. Besides that, all the little incidentals have gone down. We don't even use as much laundry soap as we used to! And the clothes are always clean, not to mention the house.''

''But you work so much,'' she protested in confusion.

''I have to get ready for the school year,'' he explained. ''Yancy and Sweetums will have to go into full-time nursery school, and then there's after-school care for Red and Chaz and all the important stuff that takes extra money and keeps me from being able to work these long hours, stuff like ball games and band instruments and PTA meetings.... Mattie, you don't realize it, but you've given me my first chance to get ahead since I started doing this all on my own. That's why I want your advice now. What do you think? It's a long-term project, you know. Because of the cost of the bull, we'd only be able to buy a single heifer to start.''

Mattie got up from her chair and opened the drawer where she kept the few tools one always needed around a house. Extracting a small hammer she said, ''I think we'd better go take down that sign before somebody takes it seriously and makes you an offer you can't refuse for that land. Can't build a ranch without land, you know.''

For a moment Orren just stared at her, something so tender in his eyes that she could barely look at it. Then Chaz whacked a fist on the table, urging, ''Do it, Dad!'' And the younger girls added their uncomprehending support, beating a hardy tattoo on the tabletop. ''Yeah! Do it! Do it! Do it!''

Orren turned a look at the only silent one in the room. ''What do you think, Red?''

Jean Marie hunched a shoulder. ''Might as well—unless you forgot to tell Santy Claus that me and Chaz gets bikes this year.''

Orren grinned. ''Bikes, it is.''

Chaz shot Jean Marie a thumbs-up sign. Orren got up and left the room. In just seconds he returned with a big claw hammer.

''Let's get at that sign.''

Chaz scrambled up, and Yancy followed suit.

"Naw, y'all stay here," Orren told them. "It's too hot out there, and it's getting on to Sweetums's nap time. Mattie's all the help I need for this." He looked at Mattie then. "When we get back, I'll help you with the dishes so you can go on home. You ought not to spend your whole Sunday here with us."

"I don't mind," she said. The truth was she felt more comfortable here in this house than she was at home anymore. Orren stepped to the door and opened it, waving Mattie through. She felt "escorted," silly as that was.

He followed her out and along the side of the carport, then fell into step beside her when they reached the grass. They walked toward the road in silence for several moments while Mattie pondered the wisdom of asking questions that weren't any of her business. She decided there would never be a better time and bucked up her courage.

"Your ex-wife left you in pretty bad shape, didn't she?"

"Financially, you mean?" Orren said. "You could say that. I'd just bought her a new car that she couldn't live without, and she took it with her when she left, but when she didn't make the payments, it was my credit that suffered. I had no choice but to pay it off. Then there were the credit card bills I didn't know about, and of course, I paid for the divorce. Suddenly I was faced with day care for four kids, one of them a baby, and a bunch of bills I hadn't counted on. It was pretty grim for a while. In fact, this summer's been the best I've had it since Grace decided that cowboy had more appeal than me."

"I find that hard to believe," Mattie said offhandedly, realizing only when he stopped just what she'd said.

"That this is the best I've had it, or that she found him more appealing than me?"

Mattie felt color rising to her cheeks, but what the heck? She hadn't exactly made a deep secret of her feelings. Then again, neither had she stated them outright. She lifted her gaze to his, shading her eyes with one hand. "Frankly, Orren, I can't imagine a man more attractive than you."

His hammer hit the ground with a *thunk,* and he stepped forward to clasp her upper arms. "Mattie." He pulled her against him, laying his chin atop her head. "I wish I could think you've had enough experience to make an honest comparison," he said softly.

Mattie stepped back again, making him look down at her. "I've had a few boyfriends," she said, "but that's not how I know."

"Then how?" He skimmed her cheek with his fingertips.

"Orren, I've only known one other single father as dedicated as you," she said. "My own." That rocked his head back. "Don't look so surprised. Where do you think a girl gets her standards for men if not from her own father?"

He put a hand to the back of his neck. "Hadn't really thought about it."

"Well, that's how it is. Either she wants a man like him or a total opposite. It so happens that my dad is a great guy. Okay, he's hard-nosed and overprotective and he's got me stuck at twelve, which is how old I was when my mother died, but deep down he's a sentimental slob, and there is nothing he wouldn't do for me or my stepmother. We're everything to him, because when he loves, he loves with his whole heart. Don't you think I can recognize that in another man when I find it?"

"Oh, Mattie," he said, reaching out for her. She dropped her own hammer, hitting his with a *tink,* and stepped into his arms. He cupped the back of her head with one hand and kissed her so thoroughly that when he was done, she found herself unsteady on her feet. He pulled her close, kissed the curve of her ear and laid his cheek against hers, saying huskily, "Girl, you scare the pants off me."

She couldn't help herself. She had to laugh. "That wasn't quite the way I planned on doing it."

He pulled back in shock. "Your daddy obviously never taught you not to play with fire."

"Yes, he did," she said solemnly, "but he taught me honesty, too, and in case it escaped your attention, I'm not playing, Orren. I came here looking for something. I just didn't know what it was until I found it."

He stared at her for a long time, and she could tell that he was taking everything she'd said very seriously. Finally he switched his gaze and licked his lips. "Mattie, I don't know what to say."

"Don't say anything," she told him, and she bent down to pick up her hammer. "When the time's right to talk again, I suppose we'll know."

He, too, retrieved his fallen hammer and hefted it carefully in his hand. Together they turned and started across the remaining yards of grass to the sign posted next to the fence. "Mattie," he said softly, as they walked, "you're older at nineteen than Gracie was at twenty-seven. In fact, you may be older than anyone else I know."

She shrugged. "I grew up fast after my mother died."

"You took over the housekeeping for you and your father, didn't you?"

"Yes, and I found I was good at it."

"No kidding."

She grinned. "It's really pretty simple, just a matter of organization."

"It's more than that," he said. "I'm the most organized shopkeeper you'll ever see, but I never could get a handle on the housework."

"The house is my shop," she explained simply.

He sent her a sharp look. "Why do the things you say sound so logical, and how come I don't think of them, too?"

She shrugged. "Don't know. I just know that the only future I've ever envisioned for myself revolved around a husband, children and a home of my own. I don't think I'm really cut out for anything else. The problem is that it's not on a career track. You can't go to an employment agency and say, 'I want a position with a hardworking, good-looking man and a houseful of little kids who will need me and love me as much as I'll need and love them.'"

He grinned, head bowed to watch his steps. "You think I'm good-looking then?"

She rolled her eyes. "Duh."

He laughed. "Want to know something?"

"What?"

"You're better looking than I thought you were at first."

They had reached the sign. It was almost as tall as she was. She leaned against the corner of it and said, "What does that mean?"

"It means," he said, hefting the hammer, "that when I quit trying to see you as some kind of child, I started seeing quite a woman."

Despite the thrill of that, she pretended relief. "Whew! Does that mean I can stop wearing all those sexy outfits meant to catch your eye?"

He narrowed his eyes, grinning, and said, "Better wear 'em all again. I didn't let myself look the first time."

She laughed, brimming with a cautious kind of hope. "I'll do that."

"Good deal. Now let's knock this sign down so I can kiss you again."

Heart tripping with more than the effort required to swing a small hammer, Mattie beat at one end while he pounded free the other. He really didn't need much help. He hit his end so hard that the nails tore right through the lumber, and the whole sign swung on the two nails holding Mattie's end. One more good whack from her and the painted, neatly lettered sign lay on the ground, splintered at her end. Orren pounded the nails down into the posts, which remained standing, then reached for her hand. "Come on."

"What about that?" she asked, indicating the downed sign as he pulled her toward the house. "It shouldn't be left to lie out like that."

"I'll get it later."

''Why not get it now?''

He sighed. ''All right, if you insist.'' He stopped so suddenly that she bumped into him. He dropped his hammer and wrapped his arms around her, saying, ''But first things first, my meticulous Mattie.''

Before she knew what was happening, his mouth was on hers again. She should have expected the jolt by now, but it still caught her unprepared. She threw her arms around his neck, hammer flying, and held on, knowing he was going to turn her inside out and end over end before he was done. He plumbed the depths of her mouth, and she opened wide to let him, undulating her tongue beneath his and slowly twisting her head side to side, pressing herself against him so tightly that after only seconds she wasn't sure where she left off and he began. Even the throbbing against her belly was difficult to define until he rocked against her, and suddenly she knew that the joining was far, far from complete. They were both trembling by the time he played it out and pulled back.

''Man, I'm glad I'm not the nineteen-year-old right now,'' he said, running his hands up and down her arms.

''Why is that?'' she asked, not certain that she had ordered her thoughts properly yet.

''Because I didn't know when to stop at nineteen,'' he said, lowering his voice. ''That's why Gracie wound up pregnant with Chaz.''

''Oh.'' She brushed her hair back from her face. ''Well, I'm not Gracie.''

''I didn't think you were.''

''And I'm nearly *twenty.*''

He chuckled. ''So you keep saying.''

''It's true.''

''Okay. But that's not what this is about.''

''Then explain it to me.''

''It's about not making the same mistake twice,'' he said.

''Meaning?''

"Meaning...I don't honestly know just where we're heading now, Mattie, but it's not to bed—yet."

She held her hair back from her face with one hand and asked, "Orren, are you saying that you won't have sex with me unless you marry me first?"

He blinked and shifted his weight from foot to foot, mouth working but no sound coming out. Finally he stopped and stared at her. He lifted a hand to the back of his neck. "Well... I guess that's what I would be saying if I could get it past my teeth. Look, I told you how it is. You scare the...hell out of me."

She laughed. "You're cute when you sweat."

"I'm not sweating!" he denied. "It's just that I'm not even used to Mattie the woman, yet, so how can I think about Mattie the wife?"

She shook her head. "No one's saying you have to," she said.

"You know I do, though."

"I hope you do," she said honestly, "but if it doesn't happen, well, there must be an Orren Ellis, Evans Kincaid hybrid out there somewhere, and if there is, he'll find me."

He stared at her for a long time. "He better keep his distance while I'm around," he said finally. He held out an arm, and she linked hers with it. They strolled toward the house.

"Listen," she said lightly, tilting her head at him, "while you're out there picking up that sign, why don't you gather in the hammers, too?"

He chuckled. "Okay."

"I have no idea where mine is, by the way," she went on, "but since you're going to be out there, anyway, you really ought to go ahead and dig up those posts, you know."

He groaned, but he was grinning. "Something tells me my life is never going to be the same."

"I'll be sure Candy's down for her nap," she said, smiling.

"I'll get the shovel."

"I'll do the dishes, too. Then I'd better go on home."

He nodded. "It's probably best."

"I'm sure it is."

"Look at us, agreeing on everything," he teased.

She left him standing in the carport and climbed the steps to the kitchen door, saying coyly, "We haven't discussed decorating the master bedroom yet."

"You shrew!" he cried melodramatically. He was laughing when she closed the door.

Jean Marie was standing beside the kitchen counter, a serious look on her face. Mattie tried to subdue her own joy, suspecting that something important was on the girl's mind, but her voice sounded light to the point of dreamy when she asked Jean Marie if she needed something. Jean Marie just shook her head.

"Has Candy Sue gone down for her nap?" she asked.

Jean Marie nodded. "She's already asleep. Must've been pretty tired out from hanging all over you this morning."

Mattie wasn't certain, but she sensed an underlying edge in Jean Marie's voice. "Red, is—"

"Don't call me that!" Jean Marie exclaimed. "That's Daddy's name for me, not yours!"

"All right," Mattie said gently. "I'm sorry if I overstepped."

Jean Marie shrugged and walked into the living room, where she plopped down on the couch. Chaz and Yancy were watching television. Jean Marie slung an arm around Yancy's neck and fixed her gaze on the television screen, whispering something out of the corner of her mouth. Yancy looked at her in surprise, then went back to watching the program. Something funny must have happened on the screen because they all laughed suddenly. Mattie shrugged and went to the sink to start the dishwater. Before long, her gaze settled on Orren through the kitchen window.

He'd taken off his shirt and was digging out the posts with the shovel. She couldn't help thinking how handsome he was, how muscular and sleek and masculine. Was this what Amy saw when she looked at Evans? It seemed odd to Mattie, but then Amy didn't think of Evans as a father, at least, not as her own father. Mattie smiled to herself. Life was odd. Sometimes it was lousy, but sometimes...sometimes it made a person just want to sing. She remembered hearing her mother and Amy, too, singing in the kitchen at times. It had made her feel...*hopeful.* And now she knew why. She started to hum. She hardly noticed when the song became words, but washing dishes had never been quite such a joy.

Chapter Seven

Laughter wafted through his dreams. Light and womanly, it filled him with joy and anticipation. The bright, shining light of a happy future blinded him to all but the woman's shadow, its glow a nimbus around her small, delicate form. Mattie. Plainspoken, organized, loving Mattie. He reached out for her. At least he thought he did. For some reason, his arms weighed tons, and moving them was next to impossible. Mattie must have experienced the same problem because suddenly she was crying. Panicked now, he made a superhuman effort—and sat up in bed, blinking at the light that spilled into his room from the hallway.

"Mattie?"

"Da-a-ady!"

Small feet pattered on the floor, then a little bundle flew at him. He shifted his feet off the bed just in time to catch her in his arms. "Yancy? Wh—" He cleared his throat. "What's the matter, honey?"

A little arm snaked around his neck; a wet face pressed against his throat. "I wan' my mommy! Wa-ah-h!" Her sobs tore at his heart, even if he couldn't quite make sense of them.

Stunned and groggy, Orren patted her little back ineffectually. "Yancy? What are you talking about, honey? You have a bad dream or something?"

Yancy Kay curled up in his lap, stuck her thumb in her mouth and tried to talk between sobs. "Ah-uh-huh-huh-wan-huh-muh-huh-huh-mah-mah-muh!"

Orren shook his head to clear it, then reached over to snap on the bedside lamp. Yancy's tear-stained face peered up at him, framed by her own arm and his chest. He smoothed back her hair, murmuring comforting sounds as he ordered his thoughts. Gradually, Yancy calmed. Orren reached down and gently pulled her thumb from her mouth.

"Now then, tell Daddy what's wrong."

She laid her cheek against his chest, saying in a small, heartbreaking voice, "I want Mommy."

A shock wave reverberated through Orren. "You want who?"

"Mommy. *My* mommy."

Orren was momentarily speechless. He couldn't seem to make sense of this. Finally, he heard himself saying, "Yancy, do you even remember your mother?"

Her soft blue eyes grew very large and liquid in her small face. She'd put her thumb in her mouth again, and her tiny fist bobbed up and down as she slowly nodded her head.

Orren studied her in the slanted light from what he thought of now as Mattie's lamp because of the unique pierced metal pail that served as its shade. Mattie. He'd been dreaming of Mattie. Again. But something told him that he must put Mattie aside for now. He pushed a hand over his face. "Tell me, sweetheart, what do you remember about Mommy?"

Yancy pulled her thumb from her mouth and in a small dreamy voice began to recite her memories. "Mommy's tall an' preddy. She 'as sof' yellow hair. An' she smells nice. An' she touch your head wif red fingersnails. An' she whisfers…" She lowered her voice to demonstrate. "'Don' wake Daddy. Shh! Shh!' An' she pu's red kisses on you face."

Orren smiled. "Yeah, Gracie was fond of lipstick and nail polish." Lipstick and nail polish, not much for a little girl to hang on to. He thought a moment. "Yancy, what brought this on?"

She shrugged a little shoulder. "I dunno."

He sighed. Why now? He'd always told the kids that if they really needed Mommy she'd come, but it had only been a way to help them feel secure. He'd heard from Grace exactly three times in the more than two years she'd been gone, not counting the half a dozen or so cards that she'd sent the kids. He had no idea where she was now, but he supposed he could always call up her in-laws, the Flattes, and pass along a message for her. She'd been sure to let him know that she'd married Sonny, the man with whom she'd left, during the National Rodeo Finals that first year out in Las Vegas. He didn't really care one way or another as long as she stayed gone. He'd rather eat dirt than have to see her, but he'd promised himself long ago that he wouldn't let his feeling about her and her desertion interfere with the kids' welfare. He looked at Yancy's little face. Wide-awake and dry-eyed now, she stared steadily up at him with her soft blue eyes.

"Yancy, what do you want Mommy for? Can you tell me?"

She shrugged again. "I jus' wanna see her."

He nodded. Well, he supposed it was natural enough for a kid to want to see an absent parent. He'd hoped and dreamed for years to see his own father after he'd walked out, but that had never happened. He hadn't even seen his mother in years and years. He didn't even know if they were still alive. God knew what might have happened to his father, but his mother had probably drunk herself to death ages ago. She'd been on the verge of it as far back as he could remember. What he wouldn't have given as a kid to have them both with him just one day, their attention fixed, for once, on their only child. If he could give that to Yancy or any of his kids, he knew he would. At least he had to try. He hugged Yancy close.

"I'll see if I can find Mommy," he said. "It may take a while, but I'll try."

Her little arm tightened about his neck, and she kissed him on the collarbone. "I loves you, Daddy."

"I love you, too, sweetheart. Think you can sleep now?"

She nodded, her thumb in her mouth, her pale, silky hair a sweet friction against his skin. He got up and carried her through the room. He switched off the hall light with his elbow as he passed it, smiling as his daughter relaxed in his arms, snuggling against him, so sure he'd keep her safe that she was already drifting down into sleep. The door to the girls' room was open. He tiptoed inside and carried Yancy to her bed. He smiled at the square of moonlight on her yellow wall. Another of Mattie's brilliant ideas. Mattie. He'd been holding thoughts of Mattie at bay, but they came to him now, one after another.

Mattie would be such a good mother, far superior to Grace. Had Mattie's presence put Yancy in mind of her mother after all this time? How would Mattie take it if Grace suddenly appeared on the scene again? He couldn't believe she'd be anything but reasonable. Mattie was nothing if not reasonable. Patient. Capable. Wise. She'd understand. Of course, she would. He only hoped that he could find Gracie. Well, he hoped he could find her for the kids' sakes. For his own, he rather hoped she'd taken a page from his father's book and fallen off the face of the earth. He still had to make the effort, though. Mattie would understand when he explained it.

He tucked Yancy into her bed, smoothed back her hair and kissed her forehead. *An' she pu's red kisses on you face.* He remembered that red lipstick, too. Gracie could be damned inventive about where she put the stuff and how she did it, but Yancy didn't need to know that. His little girl just needed to know that her mommy hadn't completely forgotten her when she'd abandoned her father.

"Good night, angel," he whispered, but Yancy was already well on her way to dreamland. Smiling, he straightened and turned away from the bed, moving toward the door. Another husky whisper halted him.

"Daddy?"

He detoured toward the purple wall, whispering, "What is it, Red?"

"Yancy okay?"

"Yeah. Go back to sleep, honey."

"She's been crying for Mom a lot lately."

"Has she? Why didn't you tell me?"

"Didn't figure you wanted to know because of—"

He thought he knew what she was going to say. He sat down on the edge of the bed. "I always want to know what's going on with my kids, Red. I've been working a lot since we got Mattie, I know, but it's only because I know I can trust her to take care of you while I do. It doesn't mean I don't love you guys. In fact, it means just the opposite."

"I know. That isn't what I meant."

He made out her shape in the darkness at the head of the bed and pulled her into a sitting position, bringing their faces close together. "What'd you mean, Red?"

She sat silently for several moments, then she whispered sharply, "I saw you kissin' her." She shrugged free and plopped back down onto her pillow.

"You saw me kissing Mattie."

"Out the kitchen window," she confirmed sullenly.

Boy, what a night this was turning out to be. Orren sighed. "We weren't exactly hiding." But he'd hoped they hadn't been seen—once he'd thought about it, anyway. "Just for the record, Red. It isn't really any of your business who I kiss or when I kiss 'em. But more to the point, my kissing Mattie has absolutely nothing to do with how I behave as a father. I'm still the same dad I always was, and that's just what I'll continue to be. When one of my kids has a problem, I want to know about it. Period. You got that?''

''Yeah.''

''Okay. Now go to sleep. I love you.'' He kissed her quickly and stood.

''What're you gonna do?'' she asked in a low voice.

''About?''

''Yancy.''

He folded his arms. ''I'm going to try to find your mother. Don't know what else I can do.'' He felt, rather than saw, her smile.

She rolled onto her side. ''That's good.''

''Uh-huh. You oughtta keep it to yourself for a bit, though,'' he said, thinking that locating Grace might well be easier said than done. ''Go to sleep now.''

''G'night.''

''Good night, darlin'. See you in the morning.''

He checked Yancy and Sweetums to be sure they hadn't been disturbed by his whispered conversation with Red, then quickly slipped from the room and down the hall. The central air-conditioning had cooled his sheets by the time he slid between them once more, but he hardly noticed.

So Red had seen him kissing Mattie. Well, he shouldn't be surprised. Chances were she'd see him kissing Mattie again sometime. He grinned at the thought. Who'd have believed that little pixie could pack such a wallop? Gracie, now, she'd been well versed in the sexual arts before he'd even met her, despite their youth, and it had been glaringly apparent from the very beginning. Somehow Mattie was no less potent. Yet, it was entirely different with her. What came naturally to Mattie seemed to have little correlation with what came naturally to Grace. He couldn't imagine two women more different. He wondered if Grace had changed, if she would come if he did find her. He didn't know what he hoped for there. One part of him wanted her to disappear for good. Another wanted his daughter to see her mother. None of Mattie's kids would ever have to look far for her, he thought, and then he smiled. Thoughts of Mattie were never far from mind.

He wondered what it would be like to have kids with Mattie. He imagined her snuggled next to him in bed, her belly huge with his baby. She'd probably complain about her back hurting and her feet swelling up and want to know if he could really find her attractive when she felt like a beached whale. He imagined Mattie's breasts after she'd had his child, heavy, yet soft and sensitive over their underlying firmness. The thought did crazy things to his body—and his heart. What was he thinking of? Lord, he already had four kids. Could he handle even one more? He knew Mattie would want to have a baby, if not with him, then with someone.

He imagined seeing Mattie around town, pregnant and glowing. With some other man's baby. And his gut twisted cold. He felt as if a weight had dropped onto his chest. He couldn't quite breathe, and he couldn't seem to feel his own heartbeat. Mattie and some other man. No way. No way could he stand that. He thought of Gracie with Sonny Flatte. The picture that flashed before his mind's eye was distasteful but not personally crushing any longer.

He couldn't even *picture* Mattie with someone else. She'd never *been* with anyone else. He knew that as surely as he knew his own name. And he knew, too, that when Mattie went to a man, he would be her one and her only. He knew he couldn't let that man be anyone but him.

Damn if he wasn't going to have to marry that girl.

He settled down to think about that, and before long he realized something important. Mattie was just exactly what he'd always wanted. She was everything his mother had not been. Wholesome. Wise beyond her years. Emotionally mature. A natural-born nurturer. Not to mention her numerous other talents. So how come he'd wound up with a Gracie instead of a Mattie the first time?

Where do you think a girl gets her standards for men?

She wants him either to be just like her father or his exact opposite.

It wouldn't be just girls, would it? Of course it wouldn't. He sat up in bed, knees draw up, and rested his arms on them. If a girl's taste in men was dictated by her experience of her father, then a boy's must be influenced by his mother. And wasn't he living proof of that? Good grief, why hadn't he realized it before? Gracie was his own mother all over again, except her addiction wasn't alcohol, it was men—or sex. Heaven help him. He saw it all now, the self-centeredness, the feints and starts at normalcy, only to derail just when you thought everything was going well. She tried. Just like his mother, Gracie did try. She just couldn't control the impulses, couldn't get past them to put others first—not her kids, not her husband, no one. No wonder finding Gracie had seemed so right. She was just what he was used to, what he'd always known. She just wasn't what he'd always wanted, and the harder he'd tried to make her into that, the more she'd rebelled. Damn.

He was twenty-eight years old, and it had taken a little slip of a young woman to make him see how he'd set himself up for failure—and what he really wanted. How'd she get so smart, his Mattie? Must be that father of hers. Could he really be like Evans Kincaid? Brother, he hoped so! For his kids' sakes, he'd try to make it so. For love's sake, he prayed Mattie was right about him, because he had no intention of letting go of her. Now or ever.

"Look who's here!"

Mattie bit back a groan and forced a smile to her face. "Hello, Brick. What a pleasant surprise."

"Surprise?" Brick sent a blank look at Evans, completely giving the game away. "Oh, uh, well, I was just driving by."

Down a dead-end street? Mattie thought, but she said nothing. Evans was already squirming quite enough.

"We, um, we were just about to watch a movie," Evans

said brightly. "But now that you're here...we could have a game of cards!" He rubbed his hands together. "How does that sound? Anybody want to play canasta?"

Brick shuffled his feet. "Uh, I don't really know how to play canasta."

"No? Well, hearts! How about hearts?"

Brick shook his head, grimacing. "I don't really play cards at all, except...poker, maybe?"

Evans's expression was more grimace than smile, but he managed to make his voice jovial. "Poker! Ha-ha. No, I don't think so. It's a cop thing. Gambling, you know."

"Oh."

Mattie stood with arms folded and watched her dear father slowly twist in the wind. He smiled and threw up his hands.

"Oh, well! Who wants to play cards, anyway? Why don't we all just...sit down."

Mattie turned and made a beeline for the only armchair in the room. Evans practically knocked her over trying to get to it himself. In the end, though, *he* wound up sitting on the couch next to Brick, Amy on his other side. Mattie bit her lips to keep from laughing when Brick slung a freckled arm across Evans's shoulders and crossed his hairy legs, pulling taut the hem of his white duck shorts and inadvertently wiping the sole of one shoe on Evans's pristine navy slacks. Evans smacked a hand at the dust mark on the side of his knee and edged closer to his wife.

"So, Brick, how's it going?"

"Fine." Brick nodded his bright orange head, up and down, up and down, up and down, like one of those nodding dogs that people put in the back windows of their cars.

Evans cleared his throat. "Been busy, have you?"

He shook his head. "Naw. Just hanging out."

Evans's smile was growing flat. He sought Amy's hand and clamped it tightly. "Mattie's been...busy," he said.

Brick nodded and nodded, his gaze switching to Mattie.

She smiled and looked at her father. What now, Dad of

mine? Evans frowned at her and jerked his head tightly in Brick's direction. She lifted her brows as if to say, *''Who me?''* Evans glared. She took pity on him. Folding her hands in her lap she said, ''How's your mother, Brick?''

''Oh, fine. She's fine.'' Nod, nod, nod.

''That's good.''

''Yeah. She likes having me home, likes making a fuss over me.'' Nod, nod. ''You know how it is.'' More nods.

Mattie glanced at her father. ''Yes, I know how it is.''

''Parents,'' Brick said, nodding and nodding. ''I keep telling her that a man's gotta do what a man's gotta do, you know.''

''Umm.''

Amy leaned forward, peered around her husband's broad shoulders and said helpfully, ''And just what is it that a man your age does these days, Brick?''

''Oh. Hangs out. You know.'' A man apparently hung out and practiced his nodding.

Amy looked at Mattie. Her eyes said, *''Bor-ring.''* Mattie looked away, disciplining a smile. Evans caught enough of the byplay to be irritated. He leaned forward and cleared his throat.

''Want to watch a movie, Brick? We were, uh, going to watch a movie.''

''Sure.'' Nod, nod. ''Maybe. What movie is it?''

Evans named an atmospheric Academy Award winner that the critics had raved about. Brick practically gagged and quickly changed the subject. ''Hey, any of you guys seen the new action flick in town?'' They shook their heads. ''No? Oh, man, it's a hoot!'' He proceeded to describe it in nodding detail, not the plot—assuming there was one—but the carnage, the exploding heads and disappearing body parts, the smashups and the weaponry. Amy's eyes glazed over in the first thirty seconds. Mattie entertained herself watching her father try to pretend interest rather than disgust. Finally Evans had all he could take. He was starting to nod himself. He popped up in the middle of the narration.

"How about a drink? Anybody thirsty? I'm parched! I'm just parched. Tea, anyone?"

"I'll get it," Amy said eagerly, not waiting for anyone to say they wanted it first.

Evans watched her disappear into the other room with a look of utter consternation on his face. He obviously wanted very much to go after her, but he looked at Mattie and he looked at Brick and he knew one or the other of them would disappear the moment he left the room. Folding his arms, he plopped back down on the couch.

Brick shifted his position and took up right where he'd left off. Mattie crossed her legs and pretended rapt interest while Evans endured. Amy came in with a tray of iced tea in glasses, rescuing them from a description of an alien life-form that spit acid on its enemies and what that did to them. Evans carried his glass over to the television and switched it on. Normally he hated the documentary-type cop shows that were so prevalent, but he snagged the first he came across and began a running commentary on it. Brick was enthralled. It was anybody's guess how long his head could stay on the end of his neck bobbing like a tennis ball in water. Amy lifted her eyebrows at Mattie over the rim of her glass and smiled. Mattie shook her head slowly side to side, determined not to laugh. Poor Dad. Torturing himself like this for nothing.

The evening dragged on interminably, with Evans thinking up one uselessly stupid idea after another to keep it going. Finally he just baldly suggested that Brick and Mattie go somewhere together. Brick was amenable. He just couldn't come up with anywhere to go. Sighing inwardly, Mattie took matters in hand. Anything to get this evening over and done with.

"I'd like some ice cream," she announced, getting to her feet. Evans looked like he wanted to kiss her and weep on her neck.

"Oh, sure, honey. That's fine. You and Brick run along. Don't worry about us old folks."

"Thanks, Dad," Mattie said drolly. "I won't forget this."

He hurriedly shook Brick's hand. "Good of you to stop by, Brick. See you again soon. Don't keep her out too late. She's been putting in long hours."

Mattie shook her head at the not-so-subtle reference to the marathon baby-sitting session of the weekend and steered Brick out through the entry hall to his car. It was a neat little convertible, entirely too fast for a knucklehead like Brick. She wasn't about to get herself killed over ice cream. She stuck out her hands. "Give me your keys."

"Huh?"

"Give me your car keys. I'm driving."

"Oh. Uh, sure. Okay." He was too busy nodding to be offended.

Mattie got in behind the wheel and started the car.

She managed to put up with two whole hours of Brick's company, not that she had his undivided attention or anything. They ran into some of his friends at the ice cream shop. They were all mostly younger than her. She sat on the fender of the car and thought about what she was going to say to her father while they threw ice at one another out of their soda cups and generally made idiots of themselves. Figuring she'd given her dad just about enough time to start congratulating himself on how well his little plan had worked, she got back in the car and prepared to leave. Brick had no choice but to leave with her.

Back in front of her house again, she got out of the car and tossed Brick his keys, then suddenly thought of a way to spike her father's guns for good. "Oh, Brick," she said, leaning over to put her elbows on the window frame, "I've been meaning to tell you something."

"Yeah?"

"It's a secret now, so keep it to yourself, will you, at least for a while?"

"Sure, Mattie." He nodded eagerly. "Whatever you say."

"The thing is, see, I think I'm getting married."

"Married?" He couldn't have been more horrified if she'd said she was shaving her head and joining a cult. He was too upset even to nod. "Holy cow, Mattie!"

"Yeah, I know, but I can't help it. I'm in love with the guy, and you know how it is."

"But *married!* Creeps, Mattie, you could be having *kids* soon!"

She laughed. "Actually, he's already got kids. Anyway, I just thought you should know in case Dad tries to get you to 'drive by' again."

"Oh. Okay. I get it. But, Mattie, are you sure about this? Married! Holy cow."

She shrugged. "Don't worry about it, Brick. I'll be fine."

"Okay." The shock was wearing off. He was nodding again. "Well, see ya."

"See ya."

He drove off in a spray of gravel, convinced, no doubt that he had narrowly escaped with his freedom. Mattie brushed her hands together. One down. One more to go.

She let herself into the house. Not at all surprised to find that her parents had retired, even though it was still early. Evans wouldn't want to face her just now, but she couldn't let the opportunity pass. She knocked on their bedroom door. Amy answered.

"Hi, honey. Enjoy your ice cream."

"Oh, sure. Can I talk to you and Dad?"

Amy looked over her shoulder, then stepped back, clearing the way. Evans was lying in bed with the covers folded down around his waist. He sat up, holding the covers in place. "Mattie. I was just about to nod off. Long day. I'm beat."

"Uh-huh. I just thought you'd want to know right away."

"Know? Know what?"

"Brick and I have decided we're going to get married."

"What?" Suddenly he was on his feet, grabbing at the bedcovers to cover himself. "Married? Are you out of your mind?"

"Well, that's what you wanted, wasn't it, Brick and me?"

"Not married! My God, Mattie, that Brick...has brick for brains!"

"But, Daddy, you keep—"

"I never thought you'd want to marry the guy! He's just someone to hang out with! Someone to..." He saw the smiles that his daughter and his wife were trying so hard to suppress. "What is this?" he demanded.

Mattie cleared her throat and licked her lips, but it wasn't any use. She couldn't keep from chuckling. "Oh, Daddy, don't you understand? I'm no more interested in hanging out than you were...before you met Amy."

He looked suddenly several shades paler. "But marriage, Mattie! There's a world of difference between marriage and hanging out. What's wrong with having a little fun with somebody your own age?"

"Nothing. It's just that people my own age are...too young for me."

"That's nonsense! You're always trying to grow up too fast! Why can't you—"

"Too late, Dad," she interrupted gently. "I'm not trying to grow up anymore. I'm there. You just don't want to see it."

"Mattie!"

"It's all right. I understand. Orren doesn't really want to let Yancy and Candy Sue grow up, either, but at least he's wise enough to know he has no choice in the matter."

"Orren!" Evans snorted. "What does that man know about fatherhood—or anything else?"

"Quite a lot, actually. And what he doesn't know, he's learning, just as you did—and still could, if you would."

"Damnation, Mattie! Don't lecture me. I'm the parent here, and—"

Mattie sighed and turned away, looking to Amy as she walked out of the room. ''You try to reason with him, will you?''

Amy nodded.

''Matilda Kincaid, you come back here!'' Evans roared, even as Amy closed the door on the sound of his voice.

Mattie went immediately to her room, then straight into the shower. She stayed there until she'd heard her father come and go again. Poor Daddy. Poor, poor Daddy.

Mattie knocked, then went on in. The kitchen and living area were uncharacteristically empty. In fact, the house felt unusually still. This did not bode well. Orren was usually at the table lingering over a last cup of coffee, ready to walk out the door almost as soon as she walked in. ''Orren?''

''Mattie? In here!''

She went through the living room and into the hall, where she nearly collided with him.

''Sorry!'' He jerked around her, swiping at the remnants of shaving cream on his face with the towel in one hand and shaking out a pair of socks with the other. ''Honey, do you know where my work shoes are?''

Mattie leaned in the doorway and watched him yank on his socks without sitting down. ''I put them in the closet.''

He shot her a grateful look. ''Of course, you did.'' He grabbed the belt lying on the dresser and started threading it through his belt loops. ''Could you get them out, please? I overslept!''

She went to the closet and bent down to pick them up. ''No kidding? I thought maybe you were training for a new Olympic event, dressing at light speed.''

''Cute.'' He dropped down onto the bed, leaving the belt unbuckled, and reached for the shoes. She handed them over.

''Rough night?''

"Oh, man." He stomped into one shoe and went for the other. "You won't believe it."

"That bad?"

He left the laces untied and popped up, snatching his cap from the knob of the closet door. "I need to tell you about it, but it'll have to wait." He kissed her quickly on the mouth and clumped by her, shoelaces flicking across the floor.

Warmed by that kiss and the endearment he'd used so casually earlier, she followed, smiling, into the living room. "What about your lunch?" She usually made him a sandwich or something.

"No time," he said, moving on into the kitchen. "Now or later." He paused at the door, explaining, "I'm taking an early lunch hour today. I have an important chore to do."

"Anything I can help with?"

He smiled down at her. "You help just by being here."

"You're sweet." She lifted her arms around his neck, leaning into him. He didn't even try to resist, taking the kiss far deeper far more quickly than she'd expected. With a groan, he pulled back.

"Gotta go. Tell the kids I love them."

"Will do."

He paused on the bottom step to kiss her quickly one more time and say, "We've really got to talk."

"Anytime."

"Later then."

"Bye."

He climbed into the truck, fumbling for his keys, and a moment later was backing out around her little coupe. She waved, smiling to herself as she considered what it might be that he wanted to talk to her about. He turned out of the drive and she pulled back inside, closing the door. When she turned around, Chaz was standing at the end of the table, grinning at her, blue eyes sparkling. He had obviously been there long enough to witness at least one of those kisses. She decided that she wasn't going to be disturbed by that. If things went as she expected them to go, he was going to see a lot more kissing around here. She smiled.

"Good morning, sleepyhead. Dad says to tell you he loves you."

"I heard."

"Good. Got anything special in mind for breakfast?"

He shook his head.

"Okay. I'll see what I can come up with."

He followed her into the kitchen proper, practically shimmering with excitement. Mattie was beginning to feel a little uncomfortable. She pulled out a broiler pan and got down the bread.

"Cinnamon or French toast?"

He shrugged. She opened the refrigerator to see how many eggs they had left, mentally calculating how many she'd need to finish out the week.

"Something go on last night?" she asked lightly. "Everyone seems to be sleeping rather late."

"Yancy cried," Chaz said.

Mattie took out the butter and closed the refrigerator door. Cinnamon toast, it was. "Oh? How come?"

He shrugged. "Don't know. Mattie, are you gonna marry Daddy?"

"She is not!"

Mattie whirled around, her mouth hanging open. The question had been shocking enough. To find Jean Marie there pugnaciously confronting Chaz for asking it was double trouble.

"What do you know about it?" Chaz demanded. "I seen them kissing at the door."

"I seen 'em out the kitchen window!" Jean Marie retorted, sticking out her tongue.

Mattie gasped. "Oh, my!"

They ignored her. "She's not gonna marry him!" Jean Marie insisted.

"You don't know!"

"Yes, I do!" She looked at Mattie, face set belligerently. "He told me last night he's gonna ask Mama to come home!"

Mattie literally reeled. "He wouldn't."

"Yes, he would! He told Yancy, too. Just ask her!"

Mattie couldn't seem to catch her breath. Chaz glared at Jean Marie and ran from the room. After a few moments Mattie got a hold on herself and managed to display some concern for making toast. Turning her back to Jean Marie she calmly began to spread butter on the bread, while inside she was quaking so hard that her bones rattled. She'd worked her way through three pieces without tearing any of them before she heard Yancy's emphatic voice shouting, "Ya-hoo, Mommy's coming home! Mommy's coming home!"

Mattie dropped the knife. Candy Sue's shrill giggle pierced her straight through the soul. "Mommy come home!" she crowed. "Mommy come home!"

She wouldn't even remember her mother, couldn't understand what she was saying, really, but suddenly Mattie's eyes blurred with tears. She was aware of Jean Marie turning and tearing from the room, but for the moment she couldn't actually think about it. She had all she could do to stay on her feet. She swayed against the edge of the counter, too stunned and wounded to do more than merely feel. She pressed her hands flat on the countertop, breathing deeply through her mouth, until finally her vision cleared and her legs felt steady again. Then she picked up the knife and resumed buttering the bread. She just wouldn't think about it, she decided. She just couldn't think about it.

Chapter Eight

Mattie answered the telephone on the first ring, trapped the receiver between her shoulder and her ear and continued peeling the apple. "Hello."

"Mattie, it's me."

She could tell from the excitement vibrating in his voice that something special was up. Gracie? She couldn't bear to think of it. She'd been telling herself all morning that Jean Marie's big news did not mean Orren was contemplating a reunion with his ex, even if she was the mother of his children. Nevertheless, the lump that rose in her throat threatened to choke her. She had to cough it away.

"Ahem. I thought you had an errand to do during lunch."

"Did. Just got back. You feeling okay?"

She wanted to ask if what Jean Marie had told her was true, but she was afraid to hear the answer. It wasn't really any of her business, anyway. He'd made no commitment to her, no promises, and even if he had entertained the notion of letting her become more to him than a mere babysitter, well, he had a right to change his mind. Maybe he thought he had to give his family another chance to reunite. Maybe he thought he owed it to his children. And maybe he did. She coughed again and said meekly, "My throat's bothering me some."

"Then this is a bad time. Okay. Don't worry about it."

As if she could do anything else. She closed her eyes and took a deep breath. "No. Uh, I want to know why you called. I'm all right. I just... Something went down the wrong way."

"You sure? Have you checked your temperature?"

"I don't have a temperature, Orren. I'm just fine. Now tell me what's up."

He paused so long that she thought he had decided not to answer. Then he said, "It's happened again. I have another diesel engine job."

A job? She put aside the paring knife and lifted her hand to hold the telephone receiver. "What's this about a job?"

He began to speak quickly, his excitement building again. "It's a bus, Dallas to Oklahoma City route. Broke down outside Marlow. The tow truck brought it here. The company's sending another bus for the passengers and a mechanic, but they need a shop and a little help. The boss has offered us the big bay after closing."

"Us?"

"Me," he said. "Me and the company mechanic. Mattie, I know it's bad timing, and I hate to ask you to stay late again, especially if you're not feeling well, but there could be seven or eight hundred dollars in this for us."

Us? She shook her head. Of course, he didn't mean him and her. He meant him and his kids, possibly him and his kids and their mother. She seriously considered telling him to forget it. She did not, after all, feel well, but her problem wasn't physical, and she had no one to blame for it but herself. She'd agreed to stay when he hadn't given her the time of day. How could she turn him down now?

"Sure. No problem," she said as lightly as she could manage. "Any idea how late you'll be?"

"None. It could be only a few hours, or it could turn into another ordeal, but I really don't think it'll be that bad."

"All right. If I'm asleep when you come in, wake me, will you?"

"You're a saint, Mattie. Thanks, babe."

"Don't skip dinner."

He chuckled. "I promise. Kiss the kids for me."

"'Kay."

"Listen, Mattie," he said in a soft voice, "about that talk..."

"We can do it later," she said a little too briskly.

"It's important. Don't want you to think I've forgotten."

"No, of course not. Well, I'd better get the kids fed. Bye now."

"Bye."

She hung up the phone and picked at the apple peel morosely. It was just as well that he was working late. She didn't think she wanted to hear what he had to tell her, anyway. She took up the knife and began chopping the apple with a vengeance.

It was almost dawn when Orren dragged himself home. He was well pleased with the night's work and the plumpness of his wallet. The unexpected diesel job went a long way toward restoring his spirits after his conversation with Sonny Flatte's mother. Evelyn didn't have much good to say about her daughter-in-law, and she didn't know how he could get in touch with Gracie or her son, but she promised to pass the word that Orren was looking for Grace to the few friends who might run across Sonny. It wasn't likely that Grace would ever turn up, but he wondered if he shouldn't wait a few days before breaking the news to Yancy and the other kids, maybe give them time to get over the impulse. On the other hand, he didn't want them to get their hopes up. He ached for them, especially Yancy, knowing she was bound to be disappointed, but he couldn't be too upset, all things considered. Still, he wanted to do the best thing.

He'd talk it over with Mattie, see if she thought he was doing the right thing by waiting to tell the kids he hadn't been able to reach Gracie. Then, he'd tell her how much he loved her and of the plans he wanted to make for their future. He anticipated her reaction keenly, even as tired as he was. He only hoped she wasn't ill. She'd sounded strange on the phone earlier, not like his Mattie at all.

He took his shoes off just inside the kitchen door and walked in his stocking feet into the living room. The house was dark and silent, but he knew it so well that he seldom bothered to switch on lights, especially if he risked waking the children by doing so. He moved swiftly through the silent living room and into the hall. By habit, he checked in on the girls first. All three were snuggled into their beds, sleeping soundly. Chaz was asleep with a book opened on his chest and a flashlight burning under the covers. Chuckling silently, Orren switched off the flashlight, marked the page in the book and set both aside. His heart sped up as he walked back down the hall to his own bedroom.

He didn't have to get all the way to the bed before he knew that Mattie wasn't there, and then he wondered why he'd thought she would be. Wishful thinking? He backtracked to the living room and switched on the light beside the couch. Mattie gasped and bolted awake, eyes wide in panic.

"Easy, sweetheart. It's just me."

"Orren!"

"You told me to wake you. Maybe I should've let you sleep, though." He frowned and reached out a hand to lay his palm against her forehead. She flinched back. "Your eyes are swollen."

She cleared her throat, her gaze falling to her lap. "Are they? Can't think why."

"You sure you're well?"

"I'm fine." She swung her feet to the floor, saying, "I'd better get home."

"Whoa. I thought we were going to talk."

Mattie grimaced and put a hand to her head. "What time is it?"

"Five-forty."

She kept her gaze down, sighing. "Orren, you're right. I don't feel at all well. I just want to go home, take something, and get some real sleep." He reached for her forehead again, but she jerked away. "Don't. It might be catching."

He frowned. "You should have told me earlier."

"Someone had to stay with the kids."

"Did you ever think you might have exposed them?" he pointed out gently.

"I kept my distance," she mumbled.

"I know," he said. "I just don't see the point in you trying to get yourself home at this time of morning when everybody here has already no doubt been exposed to whatever you might have. Go on in and get in my bed. I'll sleep out here."

She shook her head. "No, no. I'd better get home. Dad will be out looking for me if I don't."

"I'll call—"

"No, really. I just want to go home." She tossed aside the quilt she'd been sleeping under and got to her feet. "I'll see you at a quarter to ten."

"I don't have to go in until after lunch," he said. "Besides, if you're sick you need to be resting. I'll see if I can't get somebody to cover for me tomorrow."

She didn't argue with him, just slid her feet into her sandals and pushed her hair out of her face. "I'll call, let you know how I'm progressing." She moved toward the kitchen. He stood and followed her.

"Mattie, don't go."

"I have to."

"Let me—"

"Good night." She snatched her bag from the counter and was gone before he could say more. He stood staring at the closed door in the half-light, wondering just how sick she was and why it felt all wrong. Eventually his own fatigue drove him back the way he'd come. He cut off the light in the living room and moved sluggishly into the hall. A few moments later, he fell atop his bed and rolled onto his back. Sleep descended before he could do more than regret letting Mattie get away without telling her all that was on his mind.

Orren rubbed the shammy over the side of the extended cab. Not too long ago he'd considered the late-model truck an adequate vehicle for his family, even though its cramped back seat and dual buckets didn't leave a spare inch of room when they were all inside. Now, however, he saw serious shortcomings. What they really needed was room to grow, a double cab maybe or a van. Still, a truck like his always came in handy. He wondered if Mattie would be willing to trade in her coupe, or if it even belonged to her. He mentally added the topic to the growing list of subjects that he and Mattie needed to discuss.

He thought of trying to call her again. Her stepmother had said that she'd seemed "down" but that she hadn't complained of feeling ill before she'd left the house. He wondered for the dozenth time why she hadn't called as she'd said she would and where she'd gone. He'd assumed that she'd been on her way to see him and the kids, but hours had passed, and Mattie had not showed.

He finished drying the truck, squeezed out the shammy and went into the house. Chaz was sitting at the table, his chin resting atop his folded arms. "What's up, guy?"

Chaz shrugged. Orren narrowed his eyes. The boy could be coming down with whatever was plaguing Mattie. He laid a palm across the boy's forehead. It was cool to the touch. Still…

"Your throat bothering you, son?"

Chaz shrugged again. Orren pulled out a chair and sat down next to him.

"You've been kind of mopey this morning. Something bothering you?"

Chaz laid his cheek on his arm and stared at his father. "Dad, do you love Mattie?"

Orren blinked at the question, momentarily taken aback, but then he nodded. "Yes, Chaz, I do."

"Then how come you called Mama to come back?"

Orren cocked his head. He should have expected this, he realized. "Your sister tell you that?"

Chaz nodded. "Jean Marie says you ain't gonna marry Mattie 'cause you're takin' Mama back."

Orren dropped his head, shaking it side to side. "As usual, Jean Marie doesn't know what she's talking about. Son, my trying to get in touch with your mother has nothing whatsoever to do with me and Mattie. Yancy's just been feeling a little maudlin lately. She seems to think seeing your mother would make her feel better. That's the only reason I even thought about trying to find Gracie. But I wouldn't count on anything, if I was you. Nobody seems to know where she is."

"Then she ain't coming home?"

"Probably not even for a visit."

Chaz's relief was palpable. He went limp, closing his eyes and smiling. "Boy, wait'll I tell Mattie."

Orren chilled. "Mattie? Are you saying Mattie knows I was trying to get in touch with Grace?"

Chaz sat up straight in his chair. "Wasn't she s'posed to?"

For an answer, Orren groaned. "Not until I had a chance to explain!" Holy cow! No wonder she wasn't feeling well. He knew suddenly just who he had to thank for this latest fiasco. He got up from the table, roaring, "Red! Get in here!"

He was standing with his hands on his hips when a wide-eyed Jean Marie came to a stop in front of him. "What is it, Daddy?"

"Red, did I or did I not tell you to keep it to yourself that I was going to try to find your mother for Yancy?"

Her face went absolutely expressionless. "For a while, you said. How was I supposed to know how long you meant for?"

He wasn't buying. "You deliberately told Mattie before I could explain."

Her face scrunched up vehemently. "Chaz said you was going to marry her! I couldn't let her think—"

"You spiteful thing! Mattie's been good to you! She's been good to all of us! Why would you want to make her think I was taking your mama back?"

"You might!" Red insisted. "If she came back, you'd see she's a lot prettier'n Mattie!"

"Pretty is as pretty does, Red! And even if Grace was prettier than Mattie—and I don't think she is!—Grace doesn't want to be here! She went off and left us, Red. I'm sorry, but that's the truth of it. She's not here because she doesn't want to be."

Jean Marie's eyes brimmed with tears, her chin wobbled, and her mouth turned down at the corners. Then something seemed to catch her eye, and she stepped to one side, looking past Orren and out the window over the kitchen sink. Her face registered shock and then recognition, followed swiftly by excitement. She jabbed a finger at the window. "Then what's that?" she cried.

Orren spun around in time to see a copper-colored, midsize coupe with gold rims roll out of sight up the drive. For a moment he was frozen in place, trapped by shock. That couldn't have been... He'd only gone to see Evelyn Flatte yesterday morning! But the crunch of tires on gravel just outside the carport told him that he wasn't imagining things. God in heaven!

Before he could react, Red tore past him and ripped open

the door. "Mama!" She ran down the steps and disappeared. Orren looked at Chaz.

"Mattie," Chaz whispered worriedly.

Mattie. Orren closed his eyes, thanking God that Mattie was not around just then. Not that it mattered. Mattie would understand. He'd see to that. Right now he had to deal with Grace...and Red. He looked at Chaz. "You go in the back and stay with your sisters until I call you. And don't worry about anything. It'll come right, I promise. I'm not stupid enough to let Mattie get away."

Chaz smiled. "Okay, Dad, an' don't worry about Red. She don't know nothin', but she'll figure it out, I bet."

That was a bet Orren wouldn't back, but he smiled at his son. "Go on now. It won't be long."

Chaz went out one way, and Orren went out another. Gracie was standing beside her car, bent at the waist to look her eldest daughter in the face. She wore the skintight jeans and low-cut blouse that she favored, gold sandals with absurdly high heels on her feet. Her golden hair had grown longer, the back falling past her shoulders, the front and top pulled up and artfully arranged to tumble in disheveled strands around her face and in her eyes. Her mouth was as red as it could get, as red as her inch-long fingernails. Her bright blue eyes were shaded and shadowed and rimmed in black. If anything, her figure was even more voluptuous than it had been before, suspiciously so. She looked to him as if she were costumed for a play. She was unreal, a paper doll, as insubstantial as the staged and airbrushed photos in men's magazines. He felt an odd sense of relief at the realization, as if some unacknowledged part of him had worried that he would still find her attractive. He walked toward mother and daughter.

"You have your mother's eyes, anyway," Grace was saying. "You may have gotten Grandma Ellis's red hair, but that just means you'll be a red-hot honey one of these days. Ooh, yeah, I bet your daddy has to beat back the boys in a few years."

Red laughed far more ebulliently than the observation warranted. "You came right quick, Mommy," she said. "We just asked Daddy to call you night afore last."

"We?"

"Yancy and me."

"What about your brother?"

"He's inside with the girls," Orren said loudly. He looked at Jean Marie. "Red, you go on inside with the others."

"But—"

"There'll be plenty of time to visit with your mother later. Right now I want to talk to her."

Jean Marie looked to her mother for support, but Gracie was smiling at Orren, a glint in her eyes that even a kid couldn't miss. Jean Marie ducked her head and darted around her father. At the door she paused to call, "I'm glad you're here, Mommy!"

Gracie didn't answer. She was too busy posing for Orren. "You didn't think I'd be lookin' this good, did you, sugar?"

Orren smiled to himself. "Breast implants, Gracie?"

She flicked hair out of her eyes with her fingertips but didn't bother to deny it. "Only good thing Sonny Flatte ever did for me."

Orren couldn't help chuckling. "What good thing did you do for him, Grace?"

She lifted her chin and folded her arms, emphasizing the cleavage exposed by the neckline of her blouse. "I left my family for him. I walked away from everything I loved—"

Orren laughed outright. "Honey, you ought to go on the stage."

Outrage flashed in her eyes, but she muted it, saying, "Funny you should mention that. I met a Hollywood producer not too long ago, and he—"

Orren held up both hands. "Let me guess. You missed your babies so much you turned down the next Academy Award winner to rush right to them."

Confusion, guilt and wariness mixed on her face, and suddenly Orren knew that just the opposite was true.

"Damnation. You're on your way out there. I caught you coming through! Holy cow, Grace, weren't you even going to stop and say hello to your children? You were going to drive right by, within two miles of the house, on your way to California after some pipe dream! What about Sonny? What does he think of this latest passion of yours?"

She narrowed her eyes hatefully. "Sonny Flatte was the biggest mistake I ever made. That last kid was a walk in the park compared to him."

"Shut your mouth! Don't you ever let me hear you say such a foul thing again."

"They didn't hear," she said snidely. "Besides, I did it for you. I had her for you."

"I'm well aware that you'd have preferred to abort her, but don't pretend you carried her to term out of some act of love. I told you what I'd do if you didn't."

She walked forward, sliding one arm along the top of her low-slung car, the car he had bought her when she'd agreed to carry Candy Sue to term. "Orrie," she said silkily. "Let's not fight. Can't we just be glad for what we had and enjoy this little visit? There's nothing to keep us from it. I divorced Sonny months ago. And you're still the best I ever had."

Orren folded his arms and widened his stance, cocking his head to one side. "You know something, Gracie?" he said lightly. "I used to think, no matter what your faults, nobody could touch you in bed, nobody could ever do for me what you could. It took a gal with a heart of gold and more integrity than the Marine Corps to teach me otherwise." He chuckled. "I'm a mite slow, but I do learn. So, no, Gracie, we can't 'enjoy' this visit, however brief. Just the thought of it, frankly, turns my stomach. What you can do is go in there and pretend you're glad to see your children, that you've thought of them, that you've missed them.

Then you can get on your way to California, and we can all get on with our lives.''

She took rejection with more apparent aplomb than he'd imagined she would. Her eyes narrowed to black slits, but otherwise she maintained her too-sexy-for-my-own-good demeanor. ''So you found some little drudge who shares your obsession with family.''

''Nope,'' he said. ''The truth is that a beautiful young lady with more capacity to love than I ever dreamed existed found me. Us.''

''You're going to marry her,'' she pouted.

''At first opportunity.''

She thinned her mouth in disgust. ''God, you are so boringly predictable!''

''Good,'' he said. ''Then you shouldn't have any problem guessing how I'll react if you don't watch what you say and do around here.''

She folded her arms, completely abandoning her sultry stance. ''What have you told them about me?''

''Nothing. What could I tell them? No kid needs to hear that his or her mother dresses to seduce and has the selfish morality of an alley cat in heat. I haven't told them a thing.''

She was glaring bullets at him. ''That's smart, because if you had, I'd have to tell them what a boring, self-righteous, unambitious clod their father is!''

''I'm not afraid of anything you could say, Gracie,'' he told her calmly. ''See, I'm the parent who didn't abandon them.''

She couldn't come up with a retort to that. The truth didn't leave much room for invention. He turned toward the house, expecting her to follow.

''Remember what I said. They've been hurt enough by you, Grace.'' He could feel her aiming killing looks at his back, but he couldn't have cared less. All he cared about was Mattie and his kids. For the latter, he'd tolerate Grace. He had some making up to do with Mattie. Because of his dumb job, he'd put off telling her that he loved and wanted her with every fiber of his being, not that it wasn't a good job and not that he wasn't thankful for it. But if he'd had his priorities straight, she wouldn't be out there somewhere wondering if he'd truly gotten Grace out of his system.

He opened the door and stepped up into the house, Gracie right behind him. Red was sitting on the living room sofa, hands clenched tensely in her lap. She leapt up when she saw Gracie, an almost painful eagerness on her face. Orren knew then that his baby girl was going to get her heart broken and that there was nothing he could do about it. He smiled at her, trying to telegraph her his love, while Gracie looked around her.

"Mommy," Red said, fingers twisting together. "It ain't changed much, 'cept us girls' room—we each got our own wall!—a-and Daddy's room. Mat—uh, we done it up different, only it's gonna be Chaz's room soon, 'cause Daddy's just about finished the other one. Mat—er, I figure some of the money we got lately will go for making this part bigger. Maybe puttin' in a fireplace." She skimmed a nervous look at her father.

He smiled. So Mattie was thinking of enlarging the living room and putting in a fireplace, was she? She hadn't said anything to him about it yet, but she'd hinted at it. Evidently Jean Marie didn't think it was such a bad idea if she was using it to try to impress her mother. He thought it was a pretty good idea himself, and he'd tell Mattie so as soon as he got a chance.

Gracie turned up her nose, saying haughtily, "Sugar, I wish you could see the hotel I stayed in in Las Vegas. You've never seen anything like it. They put silk on the walls and gold on the toilet fixtures. We stayed there about two months."

Red looked as though she'd been punched. Orren moved to her side and put his arm around her. "Sounds interesting," he said to no one in particular. Then he targeted Grace with his gaze. "There's no place like home, though."

She snorted but wisely refrained from further comment. "Where's your brother and sisters?"

"I'll get them," Orren said. "Have a seat."

She was still standing when he came back in, a curious Candy Sue on his hip, a shy Yancy by one hand. Chaz followed reluctantly. Gracie ignored the other two and went straight for Candy Sue. "You little doll!" she exclaimed.

Candy Sue went to her readily enough, staring at her eyes as if fascinated, but Gracie didn't hold her long. She was getting too big to make an easy bundle, though Mattie seemed to manage her well enough. Grace dropped down onto the edge of the armchair, her jeans cutting deep crevices into her thighs.

"You must be Yancy," she said, reaching out a hand to her second daughter. Yancy nodded, stuck her thumb in her mouth and wrapped an arm around her father's leg. "Are you shy, fancy Yancy?" Gracie cooed.

Yancy turned her face away, her arm practically cutting off Orren's circulation. Red ran over to squat down next to her, whispering in her sister's ear. Yancy yanked her thumb out of her mouth and pushed at Jean Marie, yelling, "No!"

"Yancy, that's Mommy!" Red hissed urgently.

"That's enough, Red," Orren said, patting Yancy's back. "She'll come around."

"She don't even know her!" Chaz said sotto voce. Jean Marie doubled up her fist and smacked Chaz just above his left eyebrow. "Ow!"

Appalled and heartsick, Orren caught his daughter by the arm, shaking her lightly. "Stop it! This isn't some fairy tale, Red, and the truth's the truth. It doesn't mean we can't all sit down and have a nice visit."

She jerked away from him, tears filling her eyes. "What's the matter with y'all?" she bawled. "Mommy's home! Aren't you even glad?"

Orren shot a look at Gracie, who somehow possessed the sensitivity to appear uncomfortable. "Your mother isn't home, Red,'' Orren told her sorrowfully. ''She's here for a visit. She's on her way to California.''

''I'm going to have a part in the movies,'' Gracie said brightly.

Disbelief and horror spilled tears down Red's cheeks. She bolted from the room.

''I'll go—'' Chaz began, but Orren stopped him with a hand laid on his shoulder.

''Give her some time, son. She'll come around presently.''

Chaz nodded sagely, far too wise for his years. An awkward silence filled the room. Finally, Chaz stepped forward and politely addressed the woman who had abandoned him. ''Are you really going to be in the movies?''

Gracie preened. ''I just might! I met this man, a movie producer, and he says I've got the looks for it.''

She went on, Chaz listening attentively, and Orren had never been so proud of his son as he was in that moment. He squeezed the boy's shoulder and eased down onto the end of the couch, pulling Yancy onto his lap. Candy Sue scrambled up next to him and sprawled against his thigh. Chaz leaned against his knee. After a moment, he turned a look of such understanding and calm acceptance on his father that Orren felt his throat close. Chaz knew that his mother was a flake who couldn't hold a candle to the woman who had already replaced her in their hearts. His eyes seemed to say, too, that he'd absolved his father of any guilt or complicity in her abandonment.

I was young, Orren tried to tell him with his eyes. *I didn't know any better. But I wouldn't change it. Look what I got out of it!* He smiled and ruffled the boy's hair, so like his own. Chaz beamed back at him, and Orren knew without doubt that they were all going to be fine, even Red, once she'd accepted the inevitable. So long as Mattie understood that they loved and needed her as they'd never loved or needed anyone else but each other. He'd make her understand. God willing, he'd make her understand that they belonged together, a complete family. Forever.

Chapter Nine

The timing couldn't have been worse. But what could he do? He'd taken off the afternoon before so Mattie could have time to rest and recuperate from whatever was ailing her—and this after the boss had generously allowed him use of the big bay for the diesel job and given him the morning. If only he hadn't let Gracie stay the night before.... She had friends in the area still—like whoever passed along the word that he was trying to get in touch—she could have stayed with one of them. Yet, Grace had pleaded a desire to spend the night with her kids. Then Red had gotten that look of desperation on her face, and he'd found himself wanting to give Grace a chance to redeem herself in her daughter's eyes, even though he suspected that her desire to spend the night had as much—or more—to do with poverty than any desire to play mommy even for a night.

A closer look had revealed a Gracie worn a little ragged around the edges. Her sandals were marked up. The hems of her jeans were fraying. If he wasn't mistaken, a safety pin was holding together one bra strap in the back. The

Gracie who'd hounded him for money all those years would never have tolerated such little indignities. Obviously she now had no other choice. He'd looked in his son's knowing eyes and felt a little sorry for her. She'd left her family for nothing more than a doomed affair and a half-baked suggestion that she might find her destiny in Hollywood, provided she could get that far. He'd taken pity and okayed Red's eager offer to share half of her bed with her mother, on the condition that Gracie be gone by nine o'clock in the morning. He'd assumed that would get her out of the house before Mattie arrived.

Now here he was at six thirty-five, his shoes and socks in his hands, uniform shirt unbuttoned, belt dangling as he hurried to get to work early. The boss himself had called. What could he say? Not until I've told my baby-sitter that I love her? He cursed the luck that caused this to happen now. He was already through the living room before he realized that he had to call Mattie. Gracie would be gone by nine. Mattie usually came in between nine-thirty and nine-forty-five. He considered briefly letting the kids stay alone those few minutes until Mattie got there, but he couldn't do it. Better to explain Gracie's presence to Mattie over the telephone than risk the well-being of his children. Tragedies happened in split seconds. He simply couldn't justify leaving the kids unsupervised for up to three-quarters of an hour. He went straight to the kitchen telephone and punched in the numbers. Mattie's stepmother answered.

"Hi. It's Orren Ellis. Sorry to disturb you so early. Mattie usually picks up."

Amy Kincaid paused for what seemed an eternity before answering. "Yes, well, um, Mattie isn't taking calls this morning."

Orren felt a shiver of panic. "Is she that ill, then?"

Orren could hear someone speaking in the background: Mattie's father, he assumed. Then Amy Kincaid said, "Uh, actually, no. She, um, had a very late night last night."

A late night? With someone else? Another man? Orren gulped. Well, what could he expect after what Red had told her? He couldn't seem to wrap his mind around what to do or say next. Finally he followed the instinct to care for those he loved in any way that he could, Mattie included. "Okay," he said. "Listen, I have to go in early, but why don't we just let her sleep as long as possible? Things will be covered here until nine. Could you please tell Mattie to be here by then? I don't want my kids left alone."

"I'll see to it, Mr. Ellis."

"Thank you. A-and could you tell Mattie that I— Tell her that I missed her yesterday."

To his surprise and relief, Amy Kincaid's voice softened. "I'll tell her," she said. "I think she'll be glad to hear it."

He could have kissed Amy Kincaid. "Thank you. I...thanks."

He hung up the phone and took a moment to close his eyes in relief before going on to the next problem. Should he leave a note for the kids or wake Grace? He decided that motherhood entitled Grace to get awakened hours earlier than she'd planned, probably earlier than she'd been awakened in more than two years. He left his shoes and socks sitting on the kitchen table and headed back through the living room.

"Daddy?"

The sound of his daughter's tentative voice brought him to a whirling halt. "Red?" He took in the small form huddled beneath the old quilt on the couch. "What're you doing out here?"

She turned her face away, her wild red hair all but obscuring the wobbling chin. Orren abandoned the rush and sat down at her feet, reaching beneath the blanket to rub her small ankles.

"What's wrong, honey?" He tried a grin and teasing tone. "Mama snore or hog the covers? Maybe that's where Yancy gets it."

Red pushed her hair out of her face but didn't look at

him. In a soft, aching voice she said, "The bed was too small. Ma— *She* said I should sleep on the couch 'cause it was too short for her."

Orren nodded, saddened and disgusted. "I'm sorry, Red. I know you wanted to spend the night with her. More than that, I know you wanted her to want to spend the night with you."

Red struggled up on her elbows, tears spilling from her eyes. "Why don't she? What's wrong with me?"

Orren pulled her onto his lap. "Sweetheart, there's nothing wrong with you. The problem's inside your mama. She just doesn't seem to have feelings that she ought to. I don't know why. I *do* know that you're a fine little girl. Red, you're so smart that you scare me sometimes."

She gave him a surprised and puzzled look. "How come?"

"I'm not always sure I can keep up! It scares me a little, but it makes me awful proud, too." He smoothed down her flaming hair. "And you're beautiful, you know, one of the prettiest little girls in the whole world."

The look he expected, disbelief edged with disgust, didn't materialize. Instead, she very thoughtfully said, "Mattie thinks so, too."

He chuckled and hugged her tight. "And we both know how smart Mattie is!"

"She is smart, isn't she?"

"She's more than smart, Red," he told her gently. "She's wise. And she seems to have more feelings in her than anybody I've ever known."

"You got feelings, Daddy. I can tell."

Orren felt a burn in the backs of his eyes. "Can you, darlin'? I'm glad, because I don't tell you often enough how very much I love you."

"More'n Yancy and Sweetums?" she asked in a small voice.

"No," he told her gently. "It doesn't work like that, Red. I don't know how to explain other than to say that I love you all the same and all different. You're my firstborn daughter, Red. Nothing and no one could ever replace you in my heart. And it's the same for Yancy and Chaz and Candy Sue, the same but different somehow."

"And Mattie," Red stated softly.

"Yes, I love Mattie, too, different from anyone else, even from the way I once thought I loved your mother."

Jean Marie nodded, then whispered, "Grace is real pretty, isn't she?"

"Yes, she is, in her way."

"Mattie's pretty, too, in her way."

"I certainly think so."

Red laid her head against his chest with a little sigh. "Mattie loves us, don't she, Dad?"

"I believe she does."

Red bowed her head. "I'm sorry I told her you wouldn't marry her."

"I know. But don't you worry about it. I'm not letting her get away. We need her. *I* need her."

Red lifted her head and laid it back against his arm, looking him in the eye. "There's something else," she said.

Orren smiled. With Red there would always be something else. "What's that?"

"I'm the one who got Yancy to cry for Mama. I just whispered at her, telling her things I thought I remembered so she'd miss them, too, until she cried."

Orren sighed. "Red, don't you know that I'd have tried to find your mother as much for you as for Yancy?"

Red shrugged. "I guess I knew it wasn't fair all along," she said.

"What do you mean by *fair?*"

"To Mattie. Mattie's a good mother," she said, "better than Grace ever could be."

Orren put a kiss in the center of her forehead. "I'm sorry, Red. I know you wanted Gracie to be everything Mattie is, but Grace is just Grace. And, thankfully, Mattie is Mattie."

Jean Marie expelled a short breath and smiled. "Guess we got the best end of that deal, huh?"

Orren laughed and hugged her. "You know it, kid. Now, come on. You need to get some rest. Gracie can rough it on the couch."

Gracie grumbled protests and finally said she couldn't get up because she wasn't dressed, at which point Orren realized that she was sleeping stark naked. But he was determined. He looked at Jean Marie. "Well, somebody has to do the dirty work," he said. "It's nothing I haven't seen before and survived, but you close your eyes, girl." Fighting a smile, Red turned her back and squeezed her eyes shut. Orren located Gracie's blouse and hauled her up into a sitting position, yanking it down over her head. She sputtered protests and slapped at his hands but he didn't have too much trouble getting it on her. Obviously it was a new experience for Gracie; no man had ever *dressed* her before. But there were limits even to Orren's bravado. He reckoned she'd grasped the sincerity of his intent and tossed her jeans to her, saying, "Get 'em on. Now."

Cursing like a sailor she struggled into the jeans under the covers while Orren held his hands over Red's ears and hissed, "Hush up. You wake the babies, you'll have to deal with them. I'm leaving for work early."

That effectively stoppered Gracie's mouth. She tossed back the covers and got up. Funny, but she didn't look nearly so good in the morning as he remembered. Her eyes were smudged with makeup, and her skin looked sallow, her hair dirty. Grace had been living hard, and it was beginning to show, whereas he imagined Mattie looked as fresh and sweet as she was every minute of every day. Then again, he was prejudiced. He shoved Gracie out into the hall, tucked Red into bed with a kiss and went out just in time to redirect Gracie when she headed toward their old bedroom. "Oh, no you don't. You're going to the couch."

Gracie glared at him. "Why should I sleep on the couch when there's a perfectly good bed in the other room?"

"I don't want you in my bed," Orren said firmly, "for any reason."

Her eyes gleamed cunningly, and she leaned into him. "What's the matter, Orrie, thinking of me alone in your bed mess up your day? We could go in together, start the day off right. Remember when—"

He pushed her away. "I stopped wanting you anywhere near me a long time ago, Grace, as you well know."

Her face hardened, and she straightened. "If you'd been more of a man," she spat, "maybe I wouldn't have had to go looking for it!"

"You'll always have to go looking for it, Grace," Orren told her lightly. "You're sick like that. You really ought to get some help."

Hissing like a cat, she drew back her hand, nails curled inward, her face absolutely venomous. Orren just shook his head. "Don't even think about marking me. I took your abuse and clamped down on my own temper when we were married in the name of peace, but that's over and done with, long past."

"The kids—"

"The kids know exactly who and what you are. They have someone to compare you with now, Grace, and you don't measure up very well."

"You're talking about the girlfriend, aren't you," she sneered, "some drudge willing to take on four kids in order to get a man!"

"I'm talking about the wonderful woman who takes care of us, the woman we all love. The woman I love more than I even knew it was possible to love. She would never put a vulnerable little girl out of her bed, Gracie, because she would know instinctively that what Red wanted to share was her need to know she's loved, her need to be wanted."

Gracie's look of confusion was, unfortunately, genuine. "All this is about me sending Jean Marie to sleep on the couch?" she asked incredulously.

"No," Orren said, "this is about you not even knowing

that your little girl needed to be with you just one night, one lousy night out of your life.'' The look on her face told him that she still didn't get it. She couldn't. She didn't possess the necessary sensitivity. It was a physical as much as a mental impossibility. And it didn't matter, not in the least. Orren sighed. ''I've got to go to work. You're to stay here until Mattie arrives, then I want you gone. You understand me, Grace? You leave before she gets here to stay with the kids and I'll have you up on charges of child endangerment.''

She lifted her chin. ''They're my kids, too, Orren.''

''Now if you only knew what that meant, I could rest easy,'' he retorted.

''I won't leave before she gets here, I swear,'' Gracie muttered through her teeth.

''See that you don't,'' he said, turning away. He glanced at his watch. Damn. He hurried away without another word.

Mattie knocked, then waited ten full seconds before letting herself in. Appropriately steeled, she slung her bag on the counter and looked around. Orren was not at the table. Neither was he in the living room. So why had he insisted that she come in early? She'd come over her father's objections but only after promising that she'd be home promptly at seven that evening—if not earlier. She wasn't certain that she wouldn't be given her walking papers that day, assuming that she'd been summoned early for that long-delayed talk. Now she didn't know what to think, with the truck gone and Orren nowhere in sight. She knew he wouldn't leave the children alone, and a strange car was parked in the drive. Had she been replaced already? Would he do that without telling her first? She couldn't believe that he would, but then where was he? She moved through the living room toward the hall with the intention of checking on the children, only to draw up short when a tall, frazzled blonde stepped into the doorway.

''Oh! I was coming to let you in.''

Mattie stared in shock at the blonde. Her low-cut blouse was wrinkled and appeared to have just been pulled on, as did her jeans. She was barefoot, and her hair looked as though she'd just lifted her head from the pillow after an arduous night.

"Orrie must have left the door open when he left," the woman purred.

"No," Mattie murmured. "I have a key."

The woman ignored that, saying, "The poor thing had to go in early, and after getting so little sleep. He always did let them take advantage of him down at that shop." She extended a graceful hand with long, red nails. "I'm Grace Ellis, by the way, and you are? I mean, I know you're the baby-sitter, obviously, but no one mentioned your name."

So this was Orren's ex-wife. She *had* been replaced. Pain slashed Mattie as she brushed her palm against Grace Ellis's, murmuring her name. "Mattie. It's Mattie."

Grace smiled insinuatingly. "Well, Mattie, you know how it is. Orrie never could say no, bless him. If he could, I'd have had to sleep somewhere else last night."

Mattie gulped. "You slept here. With Orren?"

Grace twinkled a smile at her. "Looks that way, doesn't it? Not that I'm the sort to *sleep* and tell."

Suddenly Jean Marie pushed past Gracie into the living room. "You're a liar!"

Gracie and Mattie gasped at the same time, but it was Mattie who automatically corrected the girl. "Jean Marie, you know better than to—"

"She's a liar, and I hate her!"

Mattie was more than shocked; she was in a *state* of shock and behaving by rote. "That's enough! Don't you ever speak to your mother that way again."

"She isn't my mother anymore! She's a—"

Mattie laid a hand over the girl's mouth, afraid of what she might say. It wouldn't be any worse than what she herself was thinking, but such thoughts were best left unspoken. And Jean Marie couldn't be allowed to think that such disrespect was acceptable behavior on her part. It never occurred to Mattie that Grace ought to be the one to do the correcting. It never occurred to Grace, either.

"That's enough, young lady. Not another word or I'll be having a conversation with your father come dinnertime. Now apologize." Jean Marie's eyes filled with tears. Mattie took her hand away. "She's still your mother, Red, and an adult, as well. Show a little respect."

Jean Marie's face contorted into a familiar expression of mulish rebellion, but then, unexpectedly, it softened. She swallowed hard and without looking at Grace said, "I'm sorry."

Grace acknowledged the apology with an emphatic nod. "It's not nice to call somebody a liar," she said with all the gravity of a sage.

Jean Marie turned pleading eyes to Mattie. "But she didn't sleep with Daddy last night," she said in a soft, carefully modulated voice. "She slept in my bed, and I slept on the couch."

A swell of hope made Mattie look to Grace for explanation or confirmation...something. Grace put her hands on her hips and leaned forward, glaring at Jean Marie.

"And Daddy didn't get me up and put you back in your bed *early* this morning, I suppose. I guess you're too young to wonder why." She smirked at Mattie then, and Mattie dropped her gaze to Jean Marie's face once more. What she found there caused her stomach to drop and the color to drain from her face. She could hardly breathe, let alone speak. It was then that a tiny body hurtled into the living room.

"Mommy!" Candy Sue cried, and to both women's everlasting shock, flew straight at Mattie.

Mattie couldn't react quickly enough to catch her and was nearly knocked off her feet by the impact. Chaz appeared in the doorway. "She hasn't been to the bathroom yet," he warned ominously, giving Mattie the perfect excuse to escape the room. When she returned, Candy Sue on her hip, she thought she was ready to face the woman Orren obviously could not forget, without giving away her own vulnerability. But Grace Ellis was not in the room. Chaz and Jean Marie looked up at her from the couch.

"She's changing her clothes," Chaz said lightly. "She said to tell you that Dad's already left for work."

"She's goin' to California," Jean Marie added truculently.

"Yeah, she says she's gonna be in the movies," Chaz confirmed.

Mattie blinked at them. "She's not staying?"

Jean Marie sighed dramatically. "We just told you she's goin' to California to get in the movies."

Mattie heard the door to Orren's room open and the clack of heels on the hardwood floor in the hallway. Gracie swayed in wearing the same jeans but a different blouse, a T-top so small that it looked as if it belonged on a six-year-old. "Gotta go!" she chimed gaily, wriggling her fingers at the children as she pattered across the room. "Kiss Daddy for me! Tell him I'll be in touch." She paused next to Mattie and bent to kiss Candy Sue on the cheek, leaving a lipstick print. Calling over her shoulder she said, "Thanks for the bed, Jeannie!"

Jeannie? Mattie nearly swallowed her tongue. A glance at Jean Marie revealed a similar reaction, her face nearly as red as her hair. Gracie was oblivious. Her attention was fixed on Mattie.

"You know, honey," she said in a "we girls" voice, "you're awful young to be a house drudge. Don't let Orren take advantage of you, and don't fall for his line, either. No matter what he says, he prefers his women mature, experienced and—" she glanced at Mattie's bustline and then her own "—shall we say, blessed." She patted Candy Sue's curly head and sauntered out the door without a backward glance.

Mattie tried to tell herself that what mattered was the

exit. Gracie was gone, and she'd obviously never had any intention of staying. However, the thought would not leave her that Orren preferred the ex, who had deserted him for another man, to her. She greatly feared that he simply could not resist the voluptuous Gracie, and she knew without a doubt that she could never share him. Fortunately, Candy Sue started to whine that she was hungry, and Mattie threw herself into preparing a huge breakfast for the kids, knowing that the best thing at the moment was to keep as busy as possible. She would have time enough to examine her broken heart later. Much too much time.

Orren baled out of the truck and took the stairs in one step. It had been a wildly busy day and yet had dragged by moment by moment at the same time. He couldn't wait to see Mattie, to settle things between them for good. He charged through the door and stopped. Mattie stood at the kitchen counter filling a bowl with the contents of a saucepan. She had never looked so good to him. Glancing in his direction, she carried the bowl to the table, set it down and took off her apron. "You're home," she said lightly. "Dinner's ready. I have to go."

"Go?" he echoed, momentarily taken aback.

She reached for her bag. "Yes. I'm in a hurry. Sorry." She attempted to slip by him, but he wasn't about to let her do it.

He clamped both hands down onto her shoulders. "No way."

She stood very still, head bowed. "Orren, this isn't necessary. I already know, and I don't want to talk about it."

"Know what?"

She glanced up and quickly away again. "About Grace."

"Grace! Is that witch still here? I threatened her life if she left the kids alone, but she knows damned well that I wanted her out of here the moment you arrived! It'd be just like her to stay around and make your life hell, though. If she—"

"She didn't," Mattie said, looking up suddenly. "She left within minutes after I arrived. I understand she had a previous commitment in California. She didn't say when she'd be back."

He snorted. "I'd guess never. I don't think her reception was quite what she was hoping for. She has no one to blame but herself, the fool. They gave her every opportunity, Red especially."

"The kids you mean?" Mattie asked, obviously confused.

"You should have seen it, Mattie. You know how Red is. She'd built up this idealized image of her mother, and Grace had all but destroyed it within the first half hour. But our Red's nothing if not stubborn, and when Grace begged to be allowed to stay the night, Red tried to make it into this mother-daughter slumber party thing. She offered to share her bed with Gracie. I found her crying on the couch early this morning. Grace had put her out with no thought for anything but her own comfort, said the bed wasn't big enough and Red would be more comfortable on the couch than her. I hauled her butt out and put Red back to bed, then I threatened her with child endangerment charges if she left before you got here. I realized later that I shouldn't have told your stepmom to send you in early, but I'd told Grace last night that she had to be out by nine, and I guess I was so distracted I didn't think better of it when the boss called me in."

Mattie grabbed him by the arms. "Then you didn't..." She seemed to go weak suddenly, swaying against him.

"Mattie! Sweetheart?"

"I'm all right," she said, laying her head against his shoulder. "Actually, I'm better than all right." She looked up at him and smiled. "Grace implied that you slept with her."

"That lying piece of—"

"Told you!"

Mattie spun away, he looked up to find all four of his

kids standing at the end of the dinner table. Jean Marie folded her arms and looked at Mattie.

"I told you she was lying."

"I'm sorry, Jean Marie. I should have listened instead of scolding."

Jean Marie shrugged. "That's okay. I shoulda said it more respecting the first time."

"We'll both know better next time then."

Jean Marie lifted both eyebrows and rocked back on her heels as if to say that she wasn't making any promises. Mattie laughed. It was classic Jean Marie, and Orren knew in his heart that Mattie appreciated that fact as much as he did. That was one of the reasons he loved her, but only one.

Mattie waved a hand at the table. "Well," she said, "dinner's ready. Why don't we sit down and—"

"Uh, no." Orren stepped up and turned her to face him. "I want to talk to you, and it's already been put off too long."

"But dinner—"

"Can wait," Orren said. Stepping closer, he looked down into her eyes. "Mattie, I—"

A giggle made him stop. He looked again at his children. This definitely needed to be done without an audience, especially one so avid. Orren captured Mattie's hand. "Come with me."

He pulled her past the kids and through the living room and hall into his bedroom, closing the door behind them. "Orren, dinner's getting cold," Mattie pointed out.

"I don't care. This is more important."

She folded her arms. "Really?"

"Yes, really."

"What is it then, Orren?"

"Okay, here goes." He took a deep breath. "Mattie, I love you."

He thought for a moment that she hadn't understood or—worse—that she simply didn't want to hear it. Then suddenly she threw herself at him, arms wrapping around his neck, and he knew that it was nothing more than shock that had held her back. "Oh, Orren!"

Laughing, he wrapped her close and lifted her off her feet. "I've been busting at the seams to tell you."

She pulled his head back and kissed him. "I love you, too!"

It was his turn to do the kissing, and he made a very thorough job of it, so happy he could explode. He was terribly aware of the bed and how easy it would be to lay her down on it and take this where he wanted so badly to go. But he wouldn't, because he needed to do this thing right, and he wanted her to understand that. When he couldn't bear it a moment longer, he set her on her feet and forced his breathing to slow enough that he could speak. "Mattie, I was young when I married Grace, too young. When she came up pregnant with Chaz, I didn't think twice about marrying her because I wanted a family of my own so badly, even when I was a boy wondering where my father was and why my mother couldn't stay sober long enough to look after me."

"Oh, Orren," Mattie said. "You don't owe me any explanations."

"But I want you to know how it was, so you'll understand how it is and how it has to be now."

"All right."

He licked his lips, searching for the right words. "I was too young at first to know that I'd made a mistake. I suppose that's why I fought my feelings for you so hard. I was afraid you'd make the same mistake I did. See, I knew the marriage wasn't right, but I actually thought that another baby might make Grace settle down. I talked her into Red. Didn't take me long to realize that wasn't the solution. She just didn't know how to be a mother. She didn't know how to love. To Grace, love was sex and nothing more. I started to think that maybe the kids and I would be better off without her, but Grace isn't a graceful loser. She knew I wasn't happy and that I was thinking about a divorce, so she got pregnant with Yancy to keep me with her."

"And it worked," Mattie said softly.

"What else could I do but try to make it work?" Orren asked. "I told myself that she might not be everything I wanted, but it wasn't all bad. She was always...*eager* sexually. I figured that meant something, that maybe no other woman could make that part of it better. But mostly it was the kids. Three kids are a huge responsibility."

"Four an even larger one."

"Candy Sue was pure accident," Orren told her. "Gracie was furious when she found out she was pregnant again. She wanted an abortion, but I wouldn't hear of it. She hated me for that. She only stayed until she got her figure back and could shop around for a way to go. And she had to be the one to go. If I'd tried to leave her, she'd have hung on out of sheer spite."

"So you had your freedom," Mattie said, "but you must have been very afraid of making another mistake."

"I still am," he admitted. Her expression immediately revealed fear and uncertainty. "Not like you're thinking," he went on quickly. "I don't have any doubt about my feelings for you or yours for me."

"Then it's—" she gulped "—a physical thing?"

"What? A physical thing?" Suddenly it registered. Sex. "Oh." He laughed. "No way! I mean... Mattie, I want you like I didn't even know I could want a woman. I don't have any worries about that. I only thought I loved Gracie. I know I love you. You're everything, absolutely *everything,* I've always wanted—only I've never wanted it so bad before."

It must have been the right way to put it, for she wrapped herself around him again, smiling in a way she hadn't ever quite smiled before. His heart sped up, and he decided that they both needed a taste of what the future could hold for them. He lowered his head and kissed her, putting his tongue inside to explore every crevice and cranny of her mouth. It wasn't nearly enough. He pressed against her, wanting her to know how very much he wanted her, and moved his mouth to the little hollow below her ear. The sound she made brought on a fierce hunger. He wanted to eat her up. He skimmed his mouth down her neck, nipping her with his teeth, licking with his tongue. His hand moved to her breast instinctively, and she arched against him.

"Orren!" She grasped his head and pulled it up, seeking his mouth again. He tightened his hand, not too hard, marveling at the firmness of her flesh, and she gasped into his mouth, giving his tongue access again. He was so caught up in the feel and the taste of her that he wasn't even aware that the door had opened until he felt a hand yanking him back roughly.

"Mattie!"

"Daddy!"

Orren blinked at the tall, fit, dark-haired man glaring murder at him and knew he could hardly have met Evans Kincaid under worse circumstances. He pulled himself together. "Mr. Kincaid, this isn't what you think."

"Isn't what I think?" Kincaid repeated incredulously. "Even your kids know what was going on in here!"

"No, sir. Well, that is, they might. I mean, they know how I feel about Mattie. They probably realize I want to—"

"Seduce my daughter?" Kincaid said in that same incredulous tone.

"Daddy!"

Evans Kincaid grabbed his daughter by the hand. "You're coming with me, young lady!"

"No, I'm not!"

"Yes, you are!"

Orren put his hand to his head. "Sir, why are you here?"

It was Mattie who answered. "I told him I'd be home early."

"She was crying the last time she came home from here," Kincaid accused. "I told her then that she was not to come back to this house, but she insisted the kids needed her. I told her she was to leave the instant you walked in the door. She promised she'd be home by seven. I knew something was wrong a minute after! Now she's going home!" He dragged Mattie out of the room and through the hall.

"Sir, if you would just listen," Orren began, following.

"I know what I saw!"

"Daddy, stop!" Mattie yanked free.

Orren shot a glance at his children, huddled together on the couch. How on earth was he ever going to explain all this to them? It was a problem he didn't have the luxury of considering just now. "Sir, please let me explain. I love Mattie and—"

"That's not love!" Kincaid exclaimed, pointing toward the bedroom.

"Mattie loves me," Orren went on doggedly.

"I do, Daddy," Mattie insisted. "I love him!"

"And we're getting married!" they said together. Orren looked at Mattie in surprise and relief—with just a touch of regret.

"Mattie, honey," he said, "I didn't even get a chance to ask you, but I was going to."

"I know," she said, slipping her hand into his. Behind her, the kids were staring with their mouths hanging open. She looked at her father again. "Orren and I are getting married, Dad," she said, "as soon as possible."

Evans Kincaid glanced at Orren, then set his jaw. "Over my dead body," he said, and with that he turned and stalked out of the house.

Orren groaned. "Aw, hell! Mattie, I'm sorry. I wouldn't have this happen for anything in the world."

"It doesn't matter."

"Doesn't matter? Honey, that's your father! Of course, it matters. We have to go after him, make him understand."

"No."

"But Mattie—"

"It wouldn't do any good, Orren. You don't know him like I do."

"Mattie, I can't let this happen. I couldn't live with myself if I caused a break with your father."

"It won't come to that," she assured him. "He'll go home, and Amy will calm him down."

That made sense. "All right," Orren said. "We'll give him some time to calm down, and then we'll talk to him."

She shook her head. "We won't get anywhere with him, not even with Amy's support. This is going to take more than the two of us." She bit her lip thoughtfully. Orren raked a hand through his hair, racking his brain for the answer. Suddenly, Mattie said, "I have to make a couple of phone calls."

Orren went with her into the kitchen. "Who are you calling?"

"The calvary," she said, looking up a phone number in the telephone book. "His name is Reverend Bolton Charles. He's the pastor at our church."

"You think he can help."

She picked up the telephone receiver. "Oh, yes."

He was willing to accept her judgment on the matter, but he couldn't help being curious. "That's one call."

Mattie smiled. "We have to have someone to stay with the kids," she pointed out gently. "I think this is going to be an adults-only conversation." She began punching in the numbers.

Orren nodded and took a deep breath. "I told my daughter you were brilliant."

"Our daughter," Mattie said.

He was kissing her when Bolton Charles answered his phone.

Chapter Ten

Mattie smiled and stepped back to let him in. "Don't you look delicious," she said softly, kissing him on the cheek. Orren blushed. Dressed in jeans, white shirt, sport coat and black, round-toed cowboy boots, Orren was nervous and trying hard to make a good impression. He'd had his hair cut, and he'd shaved so closely that his lower face looked half a shade lighter than the upper portion.

He bent to bring his mouth close to her ear. "Everybody here?"

She nodded and threaded her arm through his. "Come on in and let me introduce you. And smile." He tried, but it was apparently a pretty dismal effort. She stopped, bringing him to a stop beside her. Looking up into his eyes, she said, "I love you, Orren Ellis."

The smile that spread across his face then was totally spontaneous. He was amazed at the strength of his own feelings. "I love you, Matilda Kincaid-Soon-to-Be-Ellis."

She beamed, as calm as a goldfish pond. "Okay, then. Let's go do it."

He nodded and covered her hand with his own where it

rested on his arm. They strolled side-by-side into the Kincaid living room. Evans Kincaid stood in front of the fireplace mantel in full police uniform. Another man with sleek dark hair sat on the sofa. He wore a well-tailored suit and highly polished black shoes, and he looked as comfortable in Evans Kincaid's neat living room as he might in his own. A small, pretty woman with large eyes and short, light brown hair occupied an armchair at an angle to the sofa. She was dressed casually in sandals, tailored khaki shorts and a yellow camp shirt. Mattie led him there first.

"Orren, this is my stepmother, Amy. Amy, Orren Ellis."

Amy smiled up at him. "Mr. Ellis."

"Orren, please."

"It's nice to meet you, Orren. You have darling children."

"Thank you, ma'am. They can be a handful at times, but I'm proud of them."

"As you should be. They're so beautiful, especially the little one. All those blond curls!"

Orren chuckled. "That's my Sweetums. She's a real little angel. So's Yancy, the next one. You'd think she'd be jealous with her baby sister just a year behind her, but she's not. Then there's Red." He rubbed a hand against the nape of his neck, grinning. "That is, Jean Marie. I call her Red because of that hair of hers—and the temper that matches it! She's the one who keeps me on my toes, I can tell you. And Chaz..." He paused, looking for the words. "I was so young when he was born that I didn't have the faintest notion what I was doing, but somehow he's turned out just fine. Frankly, I don't know what I'd do without him. He's my good right arm, and that's saying something for an eight-year-old."

"Spoken like a proud father," Amy said, glancing at Evans.

"With kids like mine," Orren told her seriously, "a fellow can't help being proud."

Evans Kincaid cleared his throat. "Such a proud father would understand my concerns for my own daughter."

Orren turned to face him. "Oh, I do, sir. If you'll recall, I telephoned you for permission to hire Mattie at the beginning of the summer."

Evans's gaze was accusing. "You led me to believe that you understood she's too young to make these important decisions all on her own."

"That's exactly what I thought," Orren said. "It's a wonder she didn't crown both of us with a heavy skillet."

Evans huffed. "My daughter would never resort to such violence."

"Well, she'd be justified if she did," Orren drawled. "We both misjudged her shamefully. It's a wonder to me that she hasn't reshaped both our heads. I'm still amazed she fell in love with me."

Evans rolled his eyes. "Mattie falls in love at the drop of a hat!"

"Is that so?" Orren said smoothly. "I'll have to remember to drop mine every day then."

A warm, rich chuckle floated up from the couch. "You may have met your match here, Ev."

Mattie sighed. "They're as alike as two peas in a pod, Reverend."

"I see what you mean."

Orren stepped over to offer his hand to the reverend while Mattie made the formal introduction. "This is our pastor and friend, the Reverend Bolton Charles."

"Call me Bolton," the reverend said, coming to his feet and grasping Orren's hand.

"Thank you. I prefer first names myself."

"Excellent. Why don't we all take seats?" So saying, Bolton Charles waited until Mattie dropped down on the sofa, then reclaimed his place next to her. Mattie pulled Orren down on her other side. Evans stayed where he was by the fireplace, though a pair of armless wooden chairs of the sort that were commonly used for dining had been placed next to the hearth. Bolton Charles linked the fingers of both hands together and crossed his legs. "Now then," he said, "who would like to begin?"

Mattie lifted a hand timidly, the other grasping Orren's. "Orren and I are getting married," she began.

"You *think* you're getting married!" Evans snorted.

Mattie paused and began again, more forcefully this time. "Orren and I are getting married, *and* we'd like my father's blessing. He's being unreasonable, though, so we thought—"

"Unreasonable!" Evans exploded. "Merciful heaven, Mattie! He's looking for a full-time housekeeper and baby-sitter—among other things!"

"That's not true!" Orren said. "If it was, I couldn't do better than Mattie, but she's already keeping my house and looking after my kids. I don't have to marry her to get that!"

"Which brings us to the *other things!*"

"I'm in love with Mattie! I want to spend the rest of my life with her."

"I'm sure you said the same thing to your first wife," Evans retorted grimly.

Orren sighed. "I made a mistake with Gracie, and I don't deny it, but I was young, and I wanted a family of my own."

"Which is precisely Mattie's case!" Evans pointed out.

"But it isn't," Orren said, looking at Mattie. "I've never known anyone as wise as your daughter. And she tells me it's largely due to you, sir. She also tells me that she loves me because I'm so much like you. Personally, I don't see it," he muttered out of the side of his mouth.

Evans shook his head. "Neither do I! But even if it were true, it doesn't change the fact that Mattie's too young."

"Daddy, you know that Mother wasn't much older than me when the two of you married," Mattie pointed out.

"But she had benefits you didn't, Mattie. Your mother

died when you were at a vulnerable age. You didn't have the kind of female guidance that she did because of it."

"I grew up fast because of it," Mattie argued.

Evans appealed to Amy and Bolton Charles, a hand pointing at each. "How long has it been since she was wearing those outlandish costumes and starching her hair to stand straight on end? Would you call that growing up fast? Good grief, I moved here from California to get her away from some rock-and-roller with braids and nose rings!"

Mattie looked at Orren, a smile quirking at the corners of her mouth. "He was a total fake," she confided. "Even the tattoos."

Orren groaned. "Are you telling me that's what I have to look forward to?"

"I'd say it is guaranteed. In fact, I think we'll be lucky if that's the worst Red brings home before she's done."

Amy laughed. Orren groaned again, imagining the fellows who were going to be paraded through his living room in a few years, and said to Amy woefully, "And I've got three daughters!"

"So far," Mattie said meaningfully.

Orren swiveled his head so fast it nearly came off. "I knew that was coming eventually."

"Think we might have room for one or two more?" she asked softly, squeezing his arm.

"We'll make room."

Evans Kincaid erupted again. "My God, Mattie! Please tell me that doesn't mean what I think it does!"

"Why not? Daddy, you know I've always wanted children."

"I'll kill him!"

Mattie leaped to her feet. "You'll do no such thing!"

Orren jerked her back down again. "Hold on." He glared up at Evans. "Let's get one thing straight right now. Mattie and I haven't done anything to be ashamed of."

"By whose standard?" Evans snapped.

"Now, Evans," Bolton Charles cautioned.

Orren was on his feet before he realized he even intended to stand. "By *any* standard."

"So you say, but how am I supposed to know that?"

Orren shook with the effort to hold on to the last shreds of his temper. "You might try giving your daughter the credit she deserves! You don't have any reason to think particularly well of me. I'll give you that. I've made my mistakes and I own up to them. But *Mattie* is above reproach. As her father, I'd think you'd know that much anyway!"

"Meaning I don't know anything about my daughter, I suppose!"

"Doesn't look like it from where I'm standing!"

"You may not *be* standing much longer, pal!"

"You think so? We'll see who's left standing!"

"Oh, my!" Amy gasped, and suddenly Mattie was pushing between them.

"Orren, honey?"

He looked down in some confusion and barked, "What?"

Mattie shook her head and looked past him at Amy. "Didn't I tell you?"

"Good grief! In the same family?"

Mattie shrugged helplessly. Amy put the heels of both hands to her forehead, shuddering. Evans looked as confused as Orren felt. Bolton Charles uncrossed his long legs and cleared his throat. Every eye went right to him like metal shavings drawn by a magnet.

"Well, since it no longer appears that you're going to beat each other senseless, I have a thing or two to say."

Orren glanced at Evans guiltily and saw the same reflected back at him. He swallowed, feeling foolish, and looped an arm loosely about Mattie's shoulders as she leaned into him, her arm going around his waist. Bolton Charles got up, pushed back the sides of his jacket to slide his hands into the pockets of his pants and strolled into the center of the room.

"Let's work backward, shall we? Now then, Mattie's right." He pointed a finger back and forth between Evans and Orren. "You're definitely two of a kind."

Evans and Orren both opened their mouths to protest, but Amy added her weight to that of Mattie and Bolton. "He's right. Mattie told me, but I had to see it to believe it."

Evans snapped his mouth shut with a click of his teeth. Orren looked down at Mattie with new respect. "Maybe there's more to the notion than I thought."

Mattie smiled up at him. "Why do you think I love you so much? I told you before that I'd known only one other father as devoted as you." She looked at her father. "My own."

Evans sighed. "Honey, if that's true, then why can't you see that I only have your best interests at heart?"

"Oh, I do see it, Dad. Just as I saw that Orren only had Yancy's best interests at heart."

"Yancy?"

"That's my second daughter," Orren said, admitting sheepishly, "I guess I baby her too much. I just don't want her to be jealous of Candy."

"That's Sweetums," Mattie explained helpfully.

"Anyway, Mattie saw that Yancy was a little behind emotionally for her age and pointed it out to me."

"We'll be enrolling her in prekindergarten at First Church in the fall, by the way," she said to Bolton Charles. Bolton nodded. Orren scraped a hand through his hair. His baby going off to school already! He didn't even want to think about it.

"I guess we will," he said uncertainly.

"Count on it," Mattie said flatly, and Orren felt the color drain from his face. He took a deep breath.

Bolton Charles bit his lips and looked away. Evans was watching Orren and Mattie with beetled brow, as if he wasn't quite sure what he was seeing. Bolton cleared his throat again. "To get back to my comments..."

"Sorry," Mattie murmured.

Bolton waved away the apology as unnecessary and looked to Evans. "The plain fact is, Ev, they're both over eighteen. If they want to get married, they can, with or without your approval."

"So I should just accept it and shut up?" Evans asked disbelievingly.

"I didn't say that."

"Mattie's just barely past eighteen!"

"I'm almost twenty!"

"Man, if I've heard that once I've heard it a hundred times," Orren muttered.

"It's true!"

"All right, sweetheart. I'm not arguing. I was just letting your father know he's not getting anywhere with that line because I've tried it myself!"

Evans frowned. "You have?"

"Repeatedly."

Evans looked at Mattie, puzzled. Mattie shook her head. "I keep telling you—"

"I know, I know, peas in a pod!"

Amy laughed. Bolton chuckled. Mattie managed to keep it to a smile. Orren couldn't help smiling himself. "I guess maybe we're more alike that we realize," he said to Evans. "It doesn't seem too bad from my end. If I can do for my children what you've done for Mattie, I'll be more than happy, and that's a fact."

Evans pulled in a deep breath, his hands going to the back pockets of his slacks. "You're not quite what I expected," he conceded reluctantly. "But that doesn't mean I'm okay with this!" He turned his gaze on his daughter. "Mattie, what about college? You know what a store your mother set in a college degree. Don't you think she'd be upset by this?"

Mattie sighed. "Oh, Daddy, don't you see that I'm doing

exactly what mother did? She dropped out to marry you and have me. She wanted her degree, yes, but not until I was old enough to function on my own enough of the time to allow her to do justice to her studies. Her love for you and her desire to have a family came first. She didn't even know what she wanted to major in until we talked it over together! Well, that's exactly where I am. I can't seem to find a *reason* to stay in college, Daddy, not now. I'll go back someday because, of course, I'll want to set an example for my own children. But right now, Daddy, my place is with Orren."

Orren tightened his arm around her. He loved her so much that sometimes it was impossible to contain it all, and it just flowed over. "Mr. Kincaid," he said, "you referred to my first marriage a while ago, and I want to say right now that it was a terrible mistake. I can't regret it completely because that's where my children came from, but I'll admit that it was bad enough I don't want to make the same mistake again. I'd never marry again if I wasn't convinced that it was right. Sir, I know Mattie is the woman for me, the only woman for me."

"I might believe that, Ellis," Evans Kincaid said, "if you hadn't been married before, but you must have felt the same way then and you admit that was a mistake!"

Frustrated, Orren shook his head and looked at Mattie. "I just don't know what else to say."

Mattie looked at Evans. "Daddy, is there anything that would convince you?"

"If you waited until you graduated from college," he said after a moment.

Mattie closed her eyes. "I can't do that. Orren and the kids need me, and I need them."

"My children love Mattie as much as I do," Orren said softly. "I can't tell you how much she's brought to our lives already, and I just can't imagine living the next two years without her."

"Evans," Bolton Charles said, "you know what it's like to be in love as well as I do."

Evans looked at Amy. "Yes."

"Then surely you can understand why they don't want to wait."

Evans looked at Mattie. "I understand that my daughter could be making the biggest mistake of her life."

"Daddy, please..."

Orren tried one more time. "We're already a family in our hearts, Mr. Kincaid," he said. "I can't ask my children to wait another two years for their mother."

Bolton tried, too. "Of course, they'll go through premarital counseling."

Personally, Orren didn't think they needed counseling, but he bit his tongue and nodded his head. If that's what it took, he was willing.

"I hope you're wanting a real wedding," Amy said from her chair. "I'd hate to see you married without some celebration."

Mattie looked at Orren. He wanted to march her out of there and marry her that afternoon, but he let her know with a look that he'd do whatever she wanted. "Nothing too fussy," Mattie said to Amy. "I was thinking a morning service, maybe a tea-length dress, just the family and a few close friends." She looked at Orren and added, "A luncheon would be nice for the reception, nothing extravagant."

"So we're talking about a couple of months from now?"

Orren put his foot down then. "Not that long, I hope. I'd like to have it done before the summer's over."

"I agree," Mattie said.

Bolton injected a sour note. "I couldn't guarantee a free weekend at the church for the next month."

"Orren's off on Mondays," Mattie said.

Amy glanced at Evans, who stood with head bowed, his hands at his hips, one knee cocked slightly. "So's your father."

"A Monday it is then," Orren said before anyone could ask if Evans would actually be there at the wedding.

Bolton pulled out a pocket calendar and counted the weeks, naming a date. Orren felt as though he could finally breathe again. He pulled Mattie even closer to his side. She laid a hand over his heart and smiled up at him. He wanted to kiss her so badly, and she knew it, too! Otherwise she wouldn't have thrown that regretful look in her father's direction. He was through worrying about Evans Kincaid himself, but he'd go through all the motions for Mattie's sake.

"What about attendants?" Amy asked quietly.

"Oh, Terri, for sure," Mattie said, "and the girls, of course."

Orren chuckled. "Man, are they gonna love that!"

"Won't that be adorable," Amy said, smiling. "Think Candy's old enough to make a flower girl?"

"I think so," Orren said.

"Of course she is," Mattie agreed.

"What about you, Orren?" Amy asked. "Anyone else you want to include in the wedding party?"

Orren shrugged. "I might ask Jake to be my best man. That's my boss."

"Anyone else?"

"Not really. Just the one I think."

Bolton clicked the ink pen with which he'd been jotting notes in his pocket calendar and said, "Well, I think I just need to know one more thing. Shall we schedule the counseling sessions for Mondays as well? We'll need three."

They settled that in short order, and then there seemed nothing more to say. Orren looked around at everyone present and felt the tension building again. "I'd better be going," he said to Mattie. "I want to spend the rest of the evening with the kids."

She nodded. "All right."

He looked at Amy. "Nice to meet you, ma'am. Thanks for opening your home."

"My pleasure," Amy replied gently.

He lifted his free hand to the minister. "Reverend."

"That's Bolton."

"Bolton, I appreciate your efforts."

"Anytime," Bolton said, shaking his hand. "I expect I'll be seeing you at least a couple times a week for a while."

Orren looked at Mattie. "Yes, I've already promised Mattie. I'll be in church with her and the kids from now on."

"Good man," Bolton said. "I look forward to it."

Orren smiled and switched his gaze to Evans Kincaid. Steeling himself, Orren stepped forward and stuck out his hand again. "I appreciate you hearing me out, sir," he said. Evans looked at Orren's hand, then he looked at each one present in turn, beginning with Bolton Charles and ending with his wife. Then he walked out of the room without a word.

Mattie bit her lip and laid her head against Orren's chest. "I'm sorry, sweetheart."

"Not your fault," she said.

Amy had risen and come to them. She laid a hand on each of them. "He'll come around."

"I hope so," Orren said.

"We'll make it a matter of prayer," Bolton said. "He's a good man. He's open to God's leadership. His fears will ease."

Orren nodded and pressed a hand to the small of Mattie's back. "Walk me out, darlin'?"

"Absolutely." She turned against him, to stand at his side. Arm in arm, they left the room. At the door they paused to face each other. Orren smoothed back her hair and bent his head to kiss her. She lifted her mouth to his. He didn't let it get too involved. He didn't dare. After he lifted his head, he said, "I like your Reverend Charles."

"Everyone does."

"I can see why."

"I love you, Orren."

"Oh, sweetheart, I love you so much. And I know we're going to be okay."

She smiled for him, and he kissed her again.

He stepped out into a warm, muggy evening a few moments later and sighed. His future father-in-law hated his guts, but for some reason his future wife loved him almost as much as he loved her, and that was what counted most. He only hoped, for his love's sake, that Evans Kincaid eventually came around. Mattie deserved her father's blessing and support. If Evans was anything like him, he'd eventually understand that. Meanwhile, Orren figured he'd take a leaf from the reverend's Good Book and say a few prayers himself.

Mattie adjusted the wisp of veil that draped the brim of her wide straw hat and covered her face to the chin. She stepped back from the mirror and gave herself one more critical assessment. Her white, sleeveless, lace-covered, tea-length dress clung closely to her body, the skirt flaring just below the knees. A sweetheart neckline made the most of her bust. The simple, summery style suited her. With her long, dark hair flowing freely down her back, as Orren preferred it, she looked very much like what she was, a young, summer bride. If only her father could accept that she knew what she was doing.

She touched the small, heart-shaped, sapphire pendant that hung from a delicate silver chain around her neck. It had belonged to her mother. Amy had brought it to her only this morning, saying that Evans himself had taken the small, blue velvet box from his dresser drawer and sent it to her. Perhaps he was unbending just a bit. Perhaps he would even come, after all. She had accepted that he would not, as she had always dreamed, walk her down the aisle, but if he would just appear at the wedding, she would feel that she had not lost him. Pushing away the ripe despair that momentarily threatened to swamp her, Mattie reminded herself that she was about to marry the man of her dreams—and become a mother four times over!

As if on cue, the patter of a small herd of patent leather shoes filled the dressing room with a happy clatter. "Mommy!"

Candy Sue had taken to calling her that and throwing herself at Mattie's legs with the force of a small locomotive every time she entered a room. This time Mattie lurched forward at the waist and held out her arms to keep the little darling from ruining her white silk stockings with the buckle of her patent leather shoes. "Oh, how beautiful!"

She held off the giggling curly-top and took in the pale pink, full-skirted dress with its ruffly lace pinafore. A crown of white daisies was almost lost in the frothy curls of her pale blond hair. Yancy busily brushed down the hem of Candy Sue's skirt and handed her the tiny yellow basket that held the daisy and rose petals that she was supposed to sprinkle along the aisle of the church. Yancy had grown up so much these past few weeks. Her own pale hair had been styled in a smooth pageboy, and she wore her crown of daisies as if it was a crown of diamonds. The nosegay of pink rosebuds on her wrist remained as perfectly uncrushed as it had in the moment Amy had tied the pale yellow ribbons. Her stiffened petticoats stood out in a full circle around her thighs, and her pinafore remained as white as snow. She took her duties as bridesmaid very seriously.

Jean Marie was much more sanguine. With her wild red hair tamed into a wispy bun atop her head and her daisies pinned in place, she seemed as relaxed as if she wore shorts and a T-shirt. She carried Mattie's bouquet of daisies and pink roses nonchalantly in the crook of her arm. "Amy says it's time."

"You should see Daddy," Yancy breathed dreamily. "He looks just like a movie star!"

Jean Marie elbowed her impatiently. "You said he looked like a prince before and wanted him to wear a real crown." She rolled her eyes to make her opinion of that known before addressing herself once more to Mattie. "Chaz is waiting outside to take you to the door. I told him he didn't have to, but he says he does. Creeps, you'd think he was giving you away to some stranger, he's so nervous."

Mattie took her bouquet from her soon-to-be-daughter and composed herself. "Okay. Let's do it."

Jean Marie marched over and opened the door, while Yancy fussed with Candy Sue's hem again. Mattie curtsied slightly to Chaz, who stood stiffly in his new gray suit, white dress shirt and pale gray tie. He stuck out his arm, and she reached down to slip her hand around his bent elbow. As stately as a king going to his coronation, he stepped off. They moved down the narrow hall and into the foyer of the sanctuary. Mattie came to an abrupt halt, her heart dying away in her chest.

There in the otherwise deserted foyer, her stepmother stood with her arms thrown around a man in full-dress uniform. Mattie lifted a hand to cover her mouth. Was it...? Surely it must be! She held her breath, afraid to move or make a sound lest the vision prove a dream.

Sensing they were no longer alone, Amy withdrew and turned to face Mattie, tears streaming down her face. But Mattie had eyes only for the tall, handsome, dark-haired man at her stepmother's side. Tears sparkled in Evans Kincaid's troubled eyes.

"Mattie."

She heard a peace offering in his voice—and acceptance. Crying out, she flew into his arms. "Daddy!"

He hugged her hard, knocking her hat slightly askew. "I love you so much," he whispered.

"I love you, too! Oh, Daddy, thank you!"

After a long while, he held her apart. Tears had left wet tracks down his cheeks and clung to her own lashes. Reaching beneath the veil, he rubbed them away with the tip of his thumb. "There now. Every bit as beautiful as your mother was."

She laughed with sheer joy. A small presence at her side made her look down into Chaz's suspiciously solemn face. Mattie glanced a silent message to her stepmother. At the same time, Evans bent slightly to address the boy. "If you don't mind, son, I'll walk my daughter down the aisle."

A smile broke across Chaz's face, and he nodded, obviously glad to be relieved of the duty. Amy pulled him aside, whispering new instructions, then quickly ushering everyone into place, she and Chaz in the front of the line. Bringing up the rear, Mattie quickly straightened her hat and veil. Amy took Chaz's arm, and together they moved down the aisle. The moment Amy was in her seat, the music changed. Mattie tiptoed and peered around a corner to watch Orren's face as Chaz moved, not back down the aisle, but to the best man's side. Orren crooked a finger at him, but Chaz just gave him an okay sign and grinned.

Jean Marie began moving down the aisle, her head held high, her expression serene. When she took her place next to the altar, Yancy stepped off. She'd taken Amy's admonition about smiling to heart and was beaming like a beauty queen contestant. Mattie suppressed the urge to giggle. Yancy took her place beside her sister, and it was then that Candy Sue turned, cupped a hand around her mouth and whispered loud enough to cause titters among the guests, "Now?"

Mattie nodded and whispered back, "Yes, now."

"Okay!"

Candy Sue turned, waved at her daddy and began progressing down the aisle, step by careful step, dropping one flower petal with each movement. Mattie found it utterly charming. Then suddenly butterflies were beating their wings in her stomach. Gulping, she took a deep, deep breath and closed her eyes. In mere seconds the organist struck up the wedding march. Mattie felt an instant of sheer panic, but then her father stepped to her side and wound her arm through his. The world and all it held fell into peaceful harmony. Smiling, Mattie opened her eyes.

"Are you sure, sweetheart?"

Mattie tightened her arm around his and took a firmer grip on her bouquet. "Completely sure."

Evans nodded and together they stepped into the wide

doorway. Mattie's gaze went instantly to Orren's. She felt his shock and then his grateful pride. He adjusted his stance, shoulders squared, hands clasped, and lifted his chin. Every step of the way of that long, slow walk, he told her with his eyes how beautiful she was, how much he loved her and how happy she had made him.

When at last they drew near the altar, Evans drew a deep breath and lifted her hand from his arm. Orren extended his own hand, palm up, and Evans slowly but firmly placed Mattie's in it. Then, to everyone's surprise, Orren stepped forward and swung his free arm around Evans's shoulders in an embrace. Mattie would always remember it as the moment Evans Kincaid realized that he had not only a daughter but now also a son.

"Thank you," Orren said softly. "I promise I'll take as good care of her as she takes of me."

Evans's voice sounded a bit strangled, but his words carried clearly to all those present. "If you do that, then she'll be happy and well indeed."

They gripped each other's shoulders for a moment, and then Orren turned with Mattie to face the reverend in his formal robes, his smile wide and easy. Bolton paused for Evans to seat himself at Amy's side. Candy Sue's whisper rasped throughout the church.

"That's our gran'pa!"

Laughter hovered in the air. Bolton Charles bit his lip, lifted his eyebrows and winked at Mattie, who could only imagine her father's reaction. Amy would confirm later that he'd looked rather as if he'd been poleaxed. But by lunch he would embrace this new role with the same meticulous sense of responsibility with which he did everything. And Mattie, Orren at her side, their children around them, had at last found her own.

* * * * *